The Trevi Fountain

Sabrina made a wish, then threw a coin back over her shoulder. She turned around in time to see it splash into the fountain. Hopeful, she tried to open the magical locket. It remained locked. Sabrina peered down into the water. *That's not me!* she thought. Instead of the clothes she had on, her reflection was dressed like a Roman noblewoman.

Surprised and a little creeped out, she jumped up and almost knocked into the young man standing beside her. He'd been about to make a wish as well. Off balance, Sabrina toppled toward the pool. Before she could fall far, the young man reached out and grabbed her, then brought her to safety.

"You okay now?" he asked.

Glancing back at the fountain, Sabrina saw only her normal reflection. "Yeah, just thought I saw something in the water . . . "

Sabrina, the Teenage Witch™ books

Available from ARCHWAY Paperbacks

Sabrina The Teenage Witch™

Sabrina Goes to Rome

Written by Mel Odom
Based upon the television movie
written by Daniel Berendsen

Based on Characters Appearing in Archie Comics

And based upon the television series
Sabrina, The Teenage Witch
Created for television by Nell Scovell
Developed for television by Jonathan Schmock

AN ARCHWAY PAPERBACK
Published by POCKET BOOKS
New York London Toronto Sydney Tokyo Singapore

This book is a work of fiction. Names, characters, places and incidents are products of the author's imagination or are used fictitiously. Any resemblance to actual events or locales or persons living or dead is entirely coincidental.

AN ARCHWAY PAPERBACK *Original*

An Archway Paperback published by
POCKET BOOKS, a division of Simon & Schuster Inc.
1230 Avenue of the Americas, New York, NY 10020

Copyright © 1998 by Viacom Productions, Inc. All rights reserved.

All rights reserved, including the right to reproduce this book or portions thereof in any form whatsoever. For information address Pocket Books, 1230 Avenue of the Americas, New York, NY 10020

ISBN: 0-671-02772-7

First Archway Paperback printing October 1998

10 9 8 7 6 5 4 3 2

AN ARCHWAY PAPERBACK and colophon are registered trademarks of Simon & Schuster Inc.

SABRINA THE TEENAGE WITCH and all related titles, logos and characters are trademarks of Archie Comics Publications, Inc.

Printed in the U.S.A.

IL: 4+

s for the '98 Okies Girls' Softball team,
coached by Bill Ronne:

#00 Jillianne
#2 April
#4 Montana
#9 Natalie
#10 Megan
#11 Paula
#12 Tina
#13 Mallory
#17 Mandy
#33 Morgan
#69 Jennifer
#91 Angela
#98 Bridgette

Okies, how do you feel?

*WE FEEL GOOD, OH, WE FEEL SO GOOD!
UNH!!!*

Sabrina Goes to Rome

Prologue

Morning light from the hotel room's eastern window spilled across the antique gold locket. It was a beautiful creation, something the jeweler had intended to be proud of for the rest of his life. In fact, it had turned out to be an heirloom.

Edward Spellman turned the locket in his fingers, amazed at how heavy it was in spite of its size. He was a tall, good-looking man, but he was also a witch. He had been all his life, and he'd passed that trait on to his only daughter.

He didn't see her much these days. The divorce from her mother and his current position working for the Witches Council kept him busy traveling through other worlds than the mortal one. Though his daughter was a witch, having only come into it on her sixteenth birthday—*very much to her surprise,* he knew—he'd wanted her raised as much like a mortal as she could be. There were a lot of good things about the mortal world, and he'd been fortunate to encounter most of them. These days she lived with her aunts in Westbridge, Massachusetts.

He sat at the ornate old desk in the room's small office area. His daughter's picture sat on a corner of the desk. *She looks more like her mother every day,* he thought. And he felt good about that, too.

In the picture, his daughter held a black cat. The cat's name was Salem. Once he'd been a witch named Salem Saberhagen, who'd tried to take over the world thirty years ago. Now, thanks to a decision handed down by the Witches Council after the failed world-domination plot, Salem was a feline and his daughter's familiar. Not exactly the kind of familiar a father witch would want for his daughter. But her aunts, his sisters Zelda and Hilda, kept a close eye on things.

He turned his attention back to the locket. After all these years and all these frustrations, he still didn't want to let go of it. He remembered when it had been given to him and the challenge explained to him by his mother. She hadn't figured it out either. *I was so sure I'd be the one to figure it out,* he remembered.

That hadn't happened.

He flicked his fingernail against the locket's clasp, trying to separate the two halves. Over the years, he'd tried everything he could think of to open the locket. A hammer and chisel—one of the last resorts he'd tried—hadn't even left a mark on it.

The locket was a thing of magic and of passion, and it would take the same to open it.

Passing it on was actually a relief, though the sense of challenge remained and he wished he could have the locket for a little longer. However, the day he'd accepted the locket from his own mother he'd promised to pass it on to one of his children when they came of age.

His daughter was old enough. She'd had her first taste of love with a boy named Harvey Kinkle, who also went to Westbridge and was a member of the Fighting Scallions football team. She'd also found out love didn't always go the way she wanted it to. It was a good insight to have.

He laid the locket aside and took up the sheet of hotel stationary. He smiled when he thought of how she would act when she received the locket. It was going to be, he knew, the start of a great adventure. Since he didn't get to see her so much these days, he enjoyed sending her things, exchanging letters, and talking to her from her witches reference book, *The Discovery of Magic*. Occasionally, just to keep things more normal between them, he'd zap up a cellular phone with a faulty connection and call her.

He would have been happier, though, if the deadline didn't exist regarding the locket. In the beginning, the time had seemed like more than enough. Now it was almost gone.

He snapped his fingers and his favorite pen jumped into his hand. He wrote in flowing script:

Sabrina,
   This locket has been sealed for almost four

hundred years. In two weeks, its magic will be lost forever unless someone can open it and release the power trapped within.

He paused, looking again at the picture of his daughter, wishing he could be there while she tried to puzzle out the secret. *Mysteries,* he thought, *really are the best gifts to give kids of any age. Especially this mystery.* Who could resist such a mixture of love and tragedy? He hadn't been able to. Even his sisters had tried to figure out the locket's secret. They'd also been envious when he'd been the one chosen to keep it. Over the years, they'd contacted him with all kinds of theories regarding ways to open it.

Actually, thinking back on it, he believed it was Hilda who'd come up with the hammer and chisel idea.

He returned to his writing.

Through the centuries, everyone else in the family has tried and failed. Sabrina, now it's your turn . . .

Once he'd finished the letter, he placed the locket in the center of the paper and carefully folded the stationery around it. Then he tossed it into the air and zapped it with a pointed finger.

As important as the letter and locket were, he decided to send it special delivery. They were gone in an eyeblink and a big smile covered his face.

Sabrina's adventure in Rome had begun.

Chapter 1

☆

☆

Sabrina Spellman, teenage witch who'd traveled to the Other Realm in an eyeblink by way of the linen closet in her aunts' house, sat in the backseat of the taxi with her nose pressed to the window. The sights, spread out so casually around her, took her breath away.

Traffic filled the streets, darting here and there in an endless stream of near collisions. Car horns blared constantly, loud enough to penetrate the closed window. Outdoor cafes lounged under striped umbrellas. Shop windows caught her attention, whipping by too quickly for her to be certain what was being displayed.

Rome, she thought, *the Eternal City.*

There was something about the ring of it that just gave her goosebumps. She'd skied the red sands of Mars, gone on a date and hung out on a star, and time traveled. She'd thought maybe she'd be a little jaded. But on top of all the shopping and sight-seeing—and those items on her agenda were placed alphabetically, she'd assured her aunts—there was the gift her father had sent her.

The taxi careened past the other cars. That it didn't crash into another vehicle was a miracle. A new near miss convinced her that looking out the window was major stress she really didn't need. So she took her father's letter out of her pocket and read through it again for maybe the gazillionth time.

The secret to the locket lies in Rome.
Have a wonderful time . . .

Screeching brakes yanked Sabrina's attention from the letter. She stared through the front windshield just as the taxi driver narrowly avoided a loaded flatbed truck carrying crates of fresh fruit.

The driver looked up in the mirror and rolled his eyes like it had been the truck driver's fault. He released the steering wheel and briefly held his hands palms up, which further unnerved Sabrina as cars whizzed around them. "So sorry, *signorina.* This traffic—," he shook his head, "—how you say? Much bad!"

"Much bad," Sabrina repeated, hoping he'd grab hold of the steering wheel more quickly if she agreed. She let out a sigh of relief when he did. Then she turned her attention back to the letter. Subconsciously, she touched the cool metal of the locket hanging around her neck. She wore a short pastel plaid skirt in blues and greens, a white collarless shirt over a chartreuse cami, and platform tennis shoes. She felt properly touristy.

. . . and remember to let the magic guide you.

Love,
Dad

She folded the letter and put it back in her purse. When she'd received it and read it the first time, her imagination had gone totally rad. *Any excuse to go to Rome would have been cool,* she thought, *but to have this locket with its secret is mondo cool!*

A huge building suddenly swarmed into view ahead and on her right. She recognized it at once. It had only been featured in every vacation pamphlet she'd seen on Rome.

"The Colosseum," she said just to hear the name out loud. She found herself with her nose pressed up against the taxi window again. "I can't believe I'm in Rome."

The Colosseum looked exactly like—well, exactly the way all the pictures she'd seen showed it. Only bigger, a lot, lot bigger. It towered four stories tall with massive doors and windows Swiss-cheesed all through it. A large section of the building had crumbled down in the centuries since it had been built. But there was no denying how awesome it was.

Gladiators had fought there against savage beasts and each other for the amusement of Roman viewers. *Kind of an early version of ESPN's* Extreme Sports, Sabrina thought.

While she still had her nose pressed against the

window, knowing how uncool she probably looked to passengers in passing cars, the taxi swerved again. Knocked off balance, she slid across the seat and slammed into her big leather backpack. She hit hard enough to lose her breath for a moment.

She wasn't at all surprised when car horns honked indignantly all around them. She stayed on the backpack, getting her breath back. "How do you say *ouch* in Italian?" she asked. Then she regretted it instantly. She'd been in Rome less than an hour and she was picking up a new habit of talking to herself.

Only the bag chose to answer back. *"Aiuto.* Get off me!"

She wasn't really surprised that the bag spoke. Hanging out in the Other Realm after finding out she was a witch on her sixteenth birthday had kind of prepared her for things like that happening. However, she *hadn't* expected to recognize the voice.

She pushed herself into a sitting position. "Salem?" She opened the backpack and her familiar climbed out, stretching luxuriously.

The black cat sat and curled his tail around himself. He peered up at her with his head cocked to one side. She knew he believed it was his intelligent-but-adorable look. With a little modification, it also rapidly substituted as his *What-did-I-do?* look.

"Eight hours stuffed in an overhead bin. I'm never complaining about flying coach again," the cat declared.

Sabrina glanced at the driver, worried that he might have heard the cat talking. The driver leaned out his window and yelled at another cab that had cut him off, gesturing wildly with both hands.

Then she turned back to Salem, totally annoyed and stressed to the max. Though she loved the cat, she was also aware that he could be a major distraction and an even bigger pain. "I can't believe you stowed away."

Salem's eyes widened in surprise. "Hey, have you priced airline tickets lately? I haven't got that kind of money."

"I was *supposed* to have two catless weeks to myself."

Salem shook his head and gave her his best reproachful owl stare. "I'm hurt. I only came because I was worried about you being all alone in a foreign—" His head whipped around. "Hey, is that a pizzeria? Pull this bucket over."

Sabrina sat back in her seat and wrapped her arms around herself, giving him one of her reproachful looks. Of course, with him being Salem and tending to be self-absorbed, it didn't work. So she gave him sarcasm instead. "Your concern and your appetite are overwhelming."

Without warning the taxi hit a bump, a bone-rattling *whump!* that nearly caused Sabrina to scream as she was thrown forward. On a roller-coaster, it would have been fun—but definitely not on a taxi speeding through rush hour traffic.

Salem merely dug his claws into the seat and managed just fine.

Sabrina raised her voice to address the driver. "Excuse me, could you slow down a little? I'd like this to be my first trip to Rome, not my last."

He didn't appear to hear her, still yelling at the other cab jockeying for position alongside him now.

A large truck suddenly swerved in front of them, going *way* slower than they were. The driver didn't notice them at all.

"Watch out!" Sabrina screamed.

The driver's head snapped around and his eyes went wide as he watched the truck fill the whole windshield. There was no way they were going to miss it.

Not without help, anyway, Sabrina knew. She pointed at the taxi, hoping her spell was in time. She felt the taxi squash down, settling almost to street level. In its more aerodynamically correct form for avoiding large trucks, the taxi sped under the slower-moving truck, racing between the wheels till it reached an empty space in front. The teenage witch pointed again and the taxi sprang back to its original shape.

The driver let out a sigh of relief and turned to face his passenger. He also had his eyes open again. "See, not to worry. I'm a very good driver, no?"

"No," Sabrina agreed.

The taxi was still traveling too fast for the road conditions, rocketing toward two cargo trucks rolling side by side. And the driver was totally clueless.

"Look out!" Sabrina screamed again. Then she pointed at the taxi. The car magically squashed together from the sides, suddenly becoming a tight fit for them all. But it slid between the two cargo trucks without harm. On the other side, she turned it back to normal, thinking she should have just taken the linen closet in the Spellman home back in Westbridge. But her dad and aunts wanted her to experience the trip the way a mortal did. Her dad had felt that was part of the mindset that was needed to solve the locket's secret.

The driver glanced around at the taxi and at the traffic. He smiled at the reflection of the two trucks in the rearview mirror. He puffed out his chest a little, obviously impressed with himself. "Ah, not a scratch."

"Speak for yourself," Salem grumbled. He stayed low to the seat, his claws embedded in the seat cover.

Only a few minutes later, the taxi left the main stream of traffic and pulled into a residential area. The tall houses were everything that Sabrina had imagined about Rome. They were covered in crumbling plaster, sported colorful shutters, and all seemed determined to display a flower garden in pots on the tiled walkways and flower boxes in the windows.

Sabrina didn't even know they'd arrived until the taxi made another sharp turn and stopped quickly at the curb. She barely managed to keep her face off the seat in front of her.

"Via Badia, ventiquattro," the driver announced, waving at the house beside them.

Pulling herself up from the taxi's floorboard,

Sabrina looked out at the house. She couldn't help smiling. The place was *exactly* like she'd hoped it would be. Almost hypnotized by the exotic sight and knowing she was going to be spending two weeks there, she stepped through the door the taxi driver opened.

The shutters looked like they'd been freshly painted, and whoever tended the flowers in the boxes and pots most definitely had a mondo green thumb. She paid the driver in *lire* and gathered her suitcases and backpack. She made a show of struggling to pull her backpack on. "Wow! I guess my backpack must be putting on weight," she told the driver, who only nodded happily.

"I heard that," Salem growled from inside the backpack.

Sabrina made her way through the gate where flower vines had been woven together to make an arch. The blossoms smelled terrific. The courtyard just beyond the gate had a small, bubbling fountain, white chairs, and a microsized table with a big umbrella.

"It's perfect," she decided.

Salem shifted inside the backpack, poking his head out briefly. "I don't remember this place in the Michelin guide."

The front door banged open and the cat withdrew his head. A middle-aged woman charged through the door with an excited smile and a swirl of colorful fabric. She had dark hair and dark eyes, and showed impeccable fashion sense in her smartly cut dress.

"Buon giorno, Sabrina. Benvenuto nella mi casa!

I'm Signora Guadagno." She put her arms around Sabrina in a fierce bear hug. "We're so happy to have you here."

Sabrina felt really squished, but she felt good that the woman was so obviously excited to see her. "I'm really happy to be here."

Signora Guadagno took charge at once, talking incessantly as she pulled Sabrina into the house and gestured around at the rooms. Then they went upstairs, attacking the incline like it was some kind of welcome exercise.

Sabrina forgot to be tired, even after the footrace Signora Guadagno seemed determined to compete in. The house was beautiful, filled with dark woods and colors. The smell of baking bread hung in the air everywhere she went. Finally, the woman halted in front of a heavy carved door.

"Ah," she said, "here we are. This is your room." She opened the door, swinging it wide to reveal the well-lit bedroom beyond. Windows on two sides of the room allowed the afternoon sunlight in.

Sabrina gazed at the decor, loving it instantly. There were two beds and chests of drawers. An antique vanity with carved legs occupied one wall, a washbasin on a small table beside it. A chair sat under one window. A handmade rug decorated with flowers and vases covered the hardwood floor. A large armoire filled another wall, reaching to the tall ceiling. *This is so cool,* Sabrina thought. *I'm going to have to take lots of pictures so Libby Chessler can turn positively green with envy. And I'm going to have to take pictures of the garden and the courtyard and—*

She noticed the other girl in the room for the first time. The girl hadn't appeared aware that they'd entered the room. She looked kind of awkward standing in the middle of the doorway to the bathroom fighting to open a small plastic bag. She had short-cropped chestnut hair and wore khaki shorts and a U2 concert tank top.

"And this is your roommate, Gwen," Signora Guadagno went on, gesturing at the girl.

Startled, Gwen looked up and screamed. The extra surge of adrenaline proved to be too much for the bag she was pulling on. It ripped and spilled jelly beans in all directions. The girl stepped back and tripped over an empty suitcase left sitting out. She landed hard on the floor.

"Are you all right?" Sabrina asked.

Gwen nodded, looking more irritated than hurt.

Sabrina turned quickly to Signora Guadagno. "Roommate? I'm not supposed to have a roommate."

"Yes," Gwen said from the floor. Her accent was definitely British. "There must be some mistake."

Signora Guadagno shook her head, her smile still in place. "No mistake. I'll let you unpack and get acquainted." She stepped back out into the hallway and closed the door.

Sabrina couldn't believe it. Her father hadn't said anything about a roommate. Her aunts hadn't said anything about a roommate. She glanced back at Gwen, watching as the other girl scrambled around on her hands and knees to gather up the spilled jelly beans. She took a deep breath and

Sabrina pinned him with her gaze. "Remind me, why are you here again?"

Salem only blinked at her, knowing—finally—when to shut up.

"What else can go wrong?" Sabrina asked. Without warning, she hiccuped, clapping a hand over her mouth. "I had to ask." Hiccups weren't always just a social failing when a witch was involved. She knew that from experience. Hiccups could cause strange things to happen. She hiccuped again and walked back into the bedroom, knowing she couldn't stay in there long before Gwen got even more suspicious.

Gwen shoved clothing across the rack inside the armoire. "Let me move some of my stuff so you can unpack."

"Thanks." Sabrina hiccuped again, then watched as the table with the washbasin and vase next to the vanity floated into the air. She dashed for it, getting to it before Gwen could see it. She pushed it back down to the floor with difficulty. "I'll just stand—" She hiccuped again and the chair beneath the window started to float instead. She threw herself into it as Gwen kept working on the armoire, getting it back on the floor. "—*sit* here by the window and look at the view."

"My parents are traveling for the summer and they kind of dumped me here," Gwen said. "But it's totally fine with me because—"

Another hiccup erupted. Sabrina glanced around, wondering what had been affected now. The bed with Gwen's hamster on it started to rise.

17

And Gwen started to turn around. Sabrina threw out a leg and pushed the bed back down just in time.

"Hiccups?" Gwen asked.

"Yeah," Sabrina replied, waving at the way she sprawled across the chair and bed. "Stretching out like this helps."

"You want some water?"

"Thanks. Quickly." Gwen started for the bathroom as Sabrina hiccuped again. This time a lamp on a nightstand started floating toward the ceiling. Sabrina flailed at it with her remaining free hand and barely caught it in time.

Gwen stopped at the bathroom door. "I've got sugar in my bag if—"

"No," Sabrina interrupted, not believing the other girl hadn't noticed something was wrong. "Water. Big glass." She hiccuped again and the rug started floating. She placed her remaining foot on the rug to keep it in place. *Left hand blue, right foot on the bed*. It was hard maintaining the contortion necessary to keep everything down.

Water ran in the bathroom. "You know," Gwen called out, "sometimes it helps if someone scares you."

The next hiccup was the straw that finished Sabrina's frantic game of Witch Twister. The room's other chair floated up. Unable to reach it in time, she pointed and zapped the bathroom door locked.

Gwen pushed at the door. "Sabrina? The door. It's stuck."

Sabrina strained to hold the furniture back,

watching helplessly as the chair floated to the ceiling. Then the other furniture started pulling her up with it, shoving her relentlessly toward the ceiling. "You know these old houses are always settling," she said. "You better wait a few minutes." *Maybe I can think of something by then.* But she was clueless and helpless.

The door opened, whipping back as Gwen jumped out and shouted, "BOO!"

Chapter 2

☆

A**ll** of the floating furniture dropped back to the
floor, landing with a chorus of crashes.

Sabrina picked herself up from the floor, trying
to cover. "See, always settling. . . ."

Gwen's mouth seemed permanently frozen in an
O of surprise. She held the glass of water in her
hand.

"Hey, good call on that scaring thing," Sabrina
said. "I'll have to remember that. Is that water for
me?"

Gwen looked at her, totally stressed and shocked.
"That furniture. It was—" She struggled to find the
words.

Sabrina thought furiously, trying to figure out
what to do. Before she came up with anything, an
argument started in the corner between Salem and
the hamster.

During the confusion, the cat had slipped up on

the bed and gotten the hamster out of its cage. He batted the hamster back and forth between his paws.

"Get off me, you mangy Yankee hooligan!" the hamster yelled indignantly in a thick Cockney accent. "I swear if you try to eat me, I'll bite your bloomin' tongue off!"

Salem paused his pawing, surprised. "I've had food disagree with me before, but this is ridiculous."

Sabrina whirled on Gwen. "Your hamster—it talked!"

Gwen appeared suddenly defensive. "So did your cat!"

The nervousness and fear left Sabrina as she looked at the other girl and figured out what was *really* going on. She smiled, the hiccups forgotten now. "You're a witch."

"I am not!" Gwen pointed at Sabrina and zapped. Water drenched them both, soaking them from head to toe and pooling at their feet. "Bullocks!" She sounded totally frustrated.

"Let me guess," Sabrina said. "You tried to freeze time but didn't get the temperature setting right." She pointed at them herself, instantly drying their clothes. "Used to happen to me all the time."

Gwen glanced down at herself, running her hands across her dry clothing. She looked back at Sabrina and smiled. "You're a witch too?" She seemed enchanted by the idea. "How marvelous. Sorry about the water. I panicked."

"Maybe you should really think about cutting

21

back on the jelly beans," Sabrina suggested. Her mind was suddenly filled with all the possibilities Gwen's nature brought to light. "This is so cool. I've never met another witch who lives in this realm before."

"Hey blondie," the hamster called out, "could you call off your talking hairball?"

"No wonder I'm not a mouser," Salem said.

Sabrina glanced at the cat. "Salem, quit playing with your food. I mean, the hamster." She looked back at Gwen. "Your familiar is a hamster? How bad do you have to be to be turned into a hamster?"

"Pretty awful," Gwen answered. "His name's Stonehenge."

"I resent that remark, you blimey pathetic excuse for a witch," Stonehenge snarled.

"And my mother wonders why I have such a low self-esteem," Gwen said sadly.

Sabrina threw her arm around the other girl's shoulders. "Maybe I've got some advice regarding overly bossy familiars. Let me unpack and we'll compare notes."

Gwen nodded eagerly and they set to work. Sabrina's mood lightened considerably. At least she was no longer really alone in Rome.

"I'm sorry," Signora Guadagno apologized, "but I thought you knew. We've always taken in witches now and then to help make ends meet. Parents know, you want someone to keep an eye on your daughter while she's in Rome, send her to Signora Guadagno's."

22

Sabrina and Gwen sat around the ornate dining table in the boarding house that evening as the woman set out trays full of food. Candles gleamed and reflected from the silverware. Windows let in some of the golden light that cut through the shadows draping the courtyard out back. The teenage witch looked at the food, knowing there was no way she and Gwen could eat it all.

Signora Guadagno disappeared back into the kitchen.

"And she means it," Gwen advised knowingly. "She hasn't let me out of her sight."

Sabrina shook out a napkin and put it across her lap. "Remind me to thank my aunts for the recommendation."

Signora Guadagno came charging back through the kitchen door with the sheer power of a bulldozer. Her arms were full of more plates and serving dishes. "But not to worry," she said. "I know you don't want an old woman following you around."

"Hello." Gwen sparked up, showing instant interest. "How do I sign up for that option?"

Signora Guadagno gave the girl a displeased look. "Gwen, please. I'm talking to Sabrina." She looked at Sabrina. "My son, Alberto, will be your tour guide." She looked impatiently over her shoulder. "Alberto! Where is he?" She slid a huge steaming bowl of pasta onto the table.

Salem leaped into a chair next to the table and stretched up to look into the bowl. "Somebody pinch me. I've died and gone to heaven."

"Ah, I don't care how familiar you are," Signora Guadagno stated. "No animals at my table." She picked Salem up and dropped him on the floor next to a bowl of bilious-looking cat food.

That, Sabrina thought, feeling sorry for her pet, *looks like someone's science project. The one that* didn't *survive.*

Salem sat and bowed his head, whimpering plaintively. "Somebody slap me. I'm having a nightmare."

Signora Guadagno ignored his whimpers, making final adjustments to the serving platters and bowls. "We lost our powers long ago, but we'll get them back. Some day my Alberto—" She raised her voice. "—ALBERTO!—will marry a witch. Who knows, maybe you'll be the lucky one, Sabrina." She glanced up and smiled warmly at the girls, then headed back into the kitchen.

"Yup," Sabrina said, "they'll be hearing about this all right."

Gwen leaned into her. "But you haven't seen him yet. He's really cute."

Sabrina instantly detected the interest in the other girl's voice. Gwen reminded her of Valerie, her best friend back in Westbridge. Before she could say anything, her attention was drawn to Stonehenge. Signora Guadagno had objected totally to having anything in her dining room that resembled a rat.

The hamster scampered along the baseboard to Salem. Stonehenge sniffed at the cat food, then shuddered. "Gruel for one? Sorry I can't join you, mate, but there's a manicotti up there with my name on it."

Salem regarded the hamster coldly. "I hope you choke on a pine nut."

The hamster waddled out of sight.

Before Sabrina could warn Gwen and they could search for Stonehenge, a boy entered the dining room, obviously pushed in by the person behind him. He was skinny and looked eighteen, with dark hair and dark eyes. And, like Gwen suggested, he was cute. He wore jeans and a soccer shirt pullover.

"Ah, here he is now," Signora Guadagno announced as she walked into the room behind him.

"Buona sera," Alberto said nervously. "I am sorry to be late, but I was cleaning myself."

Gwen beamed up at him.

Oh man, Sabrina thought, *she has got it bad.*

"He's still working on his English," Signora Guadagno said.

Alberto circled the table and started to sit at the side nearest Gwen. His mother froze him with a look. "No, Alberto, there, next to Sabrina."

Nodding, Alberto sat next to Sabrina. Gwen looked totally unhappy. Sabrina smiled awkwardly at Alberto, who smiled and dropped his eyes nervously. *Her aunts were* really *going to hear about this.*

Stonehenge clambered up over the table's edge, then sped between the plates and dishes with a speed Sabrina wouldn't have believed possible.

Signora Guadagno saw him and screamed. Loudly. "Ahh! *Topo! Sparisci!*" She grabbed a large spoon and swatted the hamster off the table.

Shooting through the air, Stonehenge smacked into the wall and fell to the floor next to Salem. The cat leaned down and looked at him closely. "Oh, look what just dropped in. My entree."

"Everything is ruined," Signora Guadagno wailed. "I can't believe it, a filthy rat on my table."

"Actually, he's a hamster," Gwen said defensively. "And I just gave him a wash and blow-dry this morning."

Signora Guadagno started putting all the food on the floor next to Salem. Sabrina noticed her cat's eyes light up as he watched all the food appearing.

"Now it's only fit for the cat," the woman declared, ignoring Gwen's statement. "But don't worry, I've got lots more." She went back to the kitchen.

"Stoney," Salem announced as the hamster waddled across to join him at the unexpected feast, "I think this is the beginning of a beautiful friendship."

After dinner, Signora Guadagno cut up melons and apples for dessert. Sabrina didn't know where the woman expected them to put it after the meal they'd just had. Salem was trying valiantly to finish the last of the pasta in front of him, but it was obvious he wasn't going to be able to do it. "So much pasta, so little time," the cat whined.

When the fruit bowl was placed in the center of the table, Sabrina continued with the story she'd been telling. Her aunts had told her she could trust Signora Guadagno with anything, and she had a good feeling about Gwen. *And after four hundred years, any kind of help I'm going to get is going to be welcome.*

She passed the locket to Gwen, dangling it from her fingers so it would catch the waning light of the day. "I guess it belonged to an aunt or something, but that's really all he said. My dad's not real big on information. He forgot to mention I was a witch until I turned sixteen."

Gwen took the locket and tried to open it, failing. "You really only have two weeks to try and open it?"

"Yeah. They have four hundred years and suddenly it's up to me. And people think *I* procrastinate."

Gwen passed the locket on to Signora Guadagno. The woman studied it for a moment, and the look she gave it told Sabrina she recognized it. "So," Signora Guadagno said, "you are here to open Sophia's locket. Many before you have tried, but it sounds like you will be the last."

The name caught Sabrina's attention at once. Nobody had mentioned any names to her. Even the journal she had regarding efforts in the past to open the locket didn't mention a name. "Sophia? You know about this?"

The woman nodded. "Yes. Poor Sophia. Such a sad story."

"A sad story with a happy ending, right?" Sabrina felt the mystery surrounding the locket suddenly sharpen. It was one thing to try to find a way to open a locket, but it was another to know that a story was attached to it.

"That will be up to you," Signora Guadagno replied. "Sophia di Borgheses. She was a beautiful witch, from a powerful family."

27

"Was?" Gwen asked, hooked on the story herself. "She wasn't turned into a hamster or anything?"

"Much worse," Signora Guadagno confided in a quiet voice. "She fell in love with a mortal."

"My mother is mortal," Sabrina said. "It's not that big a deal." *Of course, there is that annoying little catch about me not seeing my mom for two years or she'll turn into a ball of wax. So okay, maybe there* are *some drawbacks.* And Harvey Kinkle was mortal. It was very possible she'd still end up sharing her life with him. At the very least, they'd always maintain a friendship.

"Perhaps," Signora Guadagno admitted. "But Sophia's love was an artist, Roberto Raoli, and he couldn't be trusted. She told him her secret and he betrayed her."

"What happened?" Sabrina asked.

Signora Guadagno handed the locket back to Sabrina. "What has to happen when you freely tell a mortal that you are a witch and he betrays you?"

Sabrina remembered the rule. It had never been a real factor in her life because she'd never really told a mortal. *At least, no one who was ever allowed to remember the fact,* she thought. Not even Harvey. She felt bad about that, but it wasn't just her secret she was protecting. She had to consider her aunts as well. "No spell can take back the truth. If he betrays your secret, you're stripped of your powers and cast out."

"No one ever saw her again," Signora Guadagno said.

Looking at the polished surface of the locket, Sabrina saw her reflection deep in the yellow gold.

She suddenly felt incredibly sad, and the locket felt heavier than ever. *That's definitely not the story I was expecting to hear.*

And there wasn't one clue about how she was supposed to open the locket.

"The one thing I hate most about being a witch—the rules," Sabrina announced. She lay on her bed in the room she was sharing with Gwen and flipped through her book, *The Discovery of Magic*. She hadn't found anything on the locket, or on Sophia di Borgheses. It was frustrating. "Most teenagers just get grounded when they screw up. We get banished."

Gwen lay on her bed as well, idly tossing jelly beans into the air. "The part I hate is trying to remember all the spells. Last week I accidentally turned myself into a white rabbit."

"Trying to fix your hair, I bet," Sabrina said. "Puns will get you every time." She flipped more pages, still finding nothing. Her head hurt from searching for information about the locket. She couldn't believe her father had dumped the locket in her lap without telling her everything there was to know about it. *And why had it turned out to be so important? I don't need that kind of pressure.*

Gwen nodded and flipped another jelly bean into the air. "Jelly bean?"

"No thanks. You know you're going to rot your teeth out."

"It's okay. I'm British." She glanced over at Sabrina. "How are you ever going to open it?"

Salem lay on a pillow nearby. Stonehenge had

crashed less than a foot away. The familiars had discovered they were kindred spirits. "Somebody grab me a hammer and a chisel and I'll pop that baby wide open," the cat offered.

Sabrina ignored him. That had been Hilda's suggestion less than an hour after she'd learned about the locket. It was written up in the thick journal Sabrina had found in the Spellman home after she received her dad's letter.

"I wrote down everything I could think of in here," she said. *Of course, everyone who's tried to solve the riddle of the locket did the same thing.* Her list had been short, and she'd found *all* of her ideas had duplicated earlier efforts. "All the places I need to go, the libraries and archives. But they wouldn't have sent me here to Rome if the answer wasn't out there somewhere," she said hopefully. "I know I can figure this out as long as I don't have any distractions."

"Well," Gwen said, "I can only think of one."

"What?"

Gwen got up from her bed and crossed the room. She threw the window open and revealed the incredible view across the rooftops around them. The sun had dipped below the horizon, leaving a last few minutes of light spread over the city, lingering like a final good-night kiss.

"Everything," Gwen said with a sigh.

Hilda Spellman moaned with pleasure.

"Did I hurt you?"

She looked up as the young masseur came around to stand in front of her. "No, Antonio, that was actually a good moan." She lay on the massage table set up in the Spellman living room.

"Oh, okay." Antonio was tall and blond and bronzed, with a buff physique from weight lifting and alligator wrestling. Hilda knew that because she'd met him a few years back when she and Zelda had vacationed down in the Everglades and had seen him wrestling alligators. She hadn't learned that he was a masseur until much later. He returned to the job at hand.

Hilda moaned again.

"That sounds dreadful," Zelda complained as she walked into the room from the linen closet.

"But it doesn't feel that way," Hilda said as Antonio worked more oil into her skin. "How was the Witches Council meeting?"

"Boring. And most of them are on diets now for the summer so lunch was a big salad buffet. I'm famished."

Hilda made a face. "Ugh. I had Andre in for lunch."

"Andre?" Zelda looked completely envious. "How did you book him?"

"I knew this two weeks was coming up," Hilda replied. "I booked ahead. You've been so busy with your projects lately, I guess you didn't think about it." Since they'd agreed to help raise Sabrina for their brother, the sisters had toned down their extravagant lifestyle. Before their niece had arrived in the house, they'd enjoyed cooks, butlers, and chauffeurs. *All* delightfully young and hunky-looking, as Sabrina would have put it. However, they'd both regretfully agreed that was no kind of environment for a young girl. She had to learn self-sufficiency and responsibility, even if she was a witch.

"I don't suppose Andre left anything from lunch?"

"Nope," Hilda replied happily.

Zelda put her hands on her hips in her big-sister reproachful attitude. Blond and vivacious, she looked beautiful in the beige pinstriped jacket-and-skirt ensemble. "It's kind of late for a massage, don't you think?"

"Oh," Hilda agreed, "it's positively sinful, but I think that's part of why it feels *so* good. I do have a reservation for you when Antonio finishes with me."

Zelda raised her eyebrows. "Maybe I was a bit hasty."

"You were. I also have Andre for dinner tonight. In fact, I have him for the whole two weeks."

Zelda sighed. "You have been extremely generous and thoughtful. I stand corrected."

"Don't stand when you can stretch out and be comfortable." Hilda zapped up another massage table. "Point up some towels and get ready for total relaxation."

Zelda did, stretching out on the other table. "Sabrina had better never find out about this."

"She's not hearing it from me," Hilda promised. Then she made a real sacrifice. "Okay, Antonio, I'm done."

"Sure," he said, moving on to Zelda.

"But only for now," Hilda told him.

The young man grinned.

When the doorbell rang, Hilda remained on the table.

"Aren't you going to get that?" Zelda asked.

"Tiberius will." Hilda watched as the young butler went to answer the door.

"You have the butler back as well?" Zelda asked in surprise.

Hilda smiled broadly. "I have them *all* back. All the household help we had before Sabrina came to live with us."

Tiberius came back to the room. His Roman-gladiator's stance and short-cropped hair were perfect. "Miss Hilda, there is a young gentleman here to see either you or Miss Zelda. His name is Harvey Kinkle."

"I'll get it," Hilda offered.

"Wasn't he supposed to cut the lawn today?" Zelda asked.

"He was supposed to, but he didn't show up." Hilda got up, zapping herself into a dark blue mini and a short-sleeved blouse that would be more appropriate for answering the door.

"Did he call?"

"No."

"That's not like Harvey."

"I know." Hilda went to the door and looked out.

Harvey Kinkle stood nervously on the stoop, looking apologetic. He wore slacks and a black T-shirt under an open plaid shirt. He smelled like cologne. "Hey, Miss Spellman," he said hurriedly,

"I know I didn't get to your lawn today and I wanted to stop by and let you know I'd get to it first thing in the morning."

"That's fine, Harvey." Hilda peered past the boy and spotted his father's car parked out at the curb. A very cute, very red-haired young girl sat in the passenger seat. "I kind of figured something must have come up."

Harvey grinned. "It's the new job I have lifeguarding at the public pool. They haven't quite got the schedules worked out yet. I worked a split shift today and there wasn't time to cut your lawn. I would've called but I was busy."

"I see." Hilda was dying to ask about the young girl in the car. But she didn't. She and Zelda had agreed to stay out of Sabrina's personal life. At least, as much as they could.

"Oh, and if Sab is still looking for a part-time job for the summer, tell her they've got a few openings down at the pool office. The hours are kind of messed up right now, but the pay's pretty good. At least you don't go home smelling like hamburger or pizza."

"She's gone right now," Hilda said. "Her father paid for a trip to Rome."

"Really? I guess she forgot to tell me. That's cool. Tell her I said to have a good time."

"Sure, Harvey. But you better get moving. I think your date's getting a little impatient."

"My date?" Harvey's eyes widened and he turned beet red. "That's just Tish. She's another lifeguard at the pool. She's kind of new in town and

34

I thought I'd show her around tonight." He looked incredibly guilty.

"Tomorrow will be fine for the lawn, Harvey," Hilda said. "You two go ahead and have fun tonight."

"Sure." Harvey turned and went back to the car.

Hilda closed the door. Harvey had been so flustered he hadn't even thought to ask about the butler. She walked back to the living room, listening to Zelda's moans of delight as Antonio massaged her. She sat in the easy chair, her appetite not quite what it had been.

"Is something wrong?" Zelda asked.

"I think Harvey's found a new girlfriend. I'm wondering how that's going to sit with Sabrina."

"They aren't exactly seeing each other these days."

"I know. But it's one thing for a guy you've been interested in to no longer date you, and it's another for him to suddenly start dating someone else."

"That's true."

"Especially a *cute* new girlfriend."

"She's cute?"

"Yes."

"How cute?" Zelda asked.

"Drop dead comes to mind."

"That cute, huh?"

Hilda nodded. "Harvey said she's new in town."

"Maybe he's just being nice."

"Looks like he had a new shirt on, and cologne."

Zelda propped herself up on one elbow. "Sabrina's the last chance any of us have at solving the mystery of Sophia's locket. She needs to concentrate on that. Two weeks will be gone before you know it."

"I was thinking about that when the household staff arrived this morning. However, now there's something else we have to consider."

"What?"

"Two weeks is plenty of time for a summer romance to happen," Hilda said. "And Sabrina's not here to figure out how she feels about that. That could be a real problem."

"Maybe we should keep an eye on things."

"Okay."

"But we're not going to tell her," Zelda said. "Whatever happens, Sabrina can deal with it when she gets back here."

"I suppose you're right."

"But?" Zelda asked. "I know I heard a *but* coming."

"I was just thinking. What if Sabrina can't solve the mystery about Sophia's locket? She's going to feel pretty bad about that. Then if she comes back and finds out Harvey's got a new romance going, that's going to be pretty hard to take."

Zelda nodded. "There's nothing we can do about it."

"I know." Hilda frowned. "There are days this parenting thing *really* bites!"

Chapter 3

☆

Sabrina studied the entry in the notebook she'd gotten concerning Sophia's locket. Though she wore the locket around her neck, she couldn't help thinking of it as Sophia's. She'd been so happy to have it when her father had sent it to her. Now it felt awkward.

No one ever saw her again. Signora Guadagno's words kept rattling around in her mind. She read the entry out loud to focus on it. "Museo Nazionale Romano. It's supposed to be on Viale delle Terme."

"I know the place," Alberto said. He walked with Sabrina and Gwen down the crowded street.

They'd taken the Metro subway earlier that morning, traveling along Line A and getting out at Barberini Station. Sabrina had lost nearly an hour while she and Gwen had taken pictures of each other posing in front of the Palazzo del Quirinale.

37

Construction on the palace had begun during the Renaissance, Alberto had informed them, and nearly every major architect at the time had contributed to the design. He'd taken their pictures in front of the huge statues of Castor and Pollux in the fountain located in the piazza. The palace had been built on the tallest of the seven hills that made up Rome, and the view of the city from there had been breathtaking.

Sabrina had forced herself to get back to work, and they'd walked west along Via della Dataria. The summer crowd was almost elbow-to-elbow the whole way. She wore tangerine drawstring cargo shorts and a high-collared sleeveless stretch white V-neck to show off her summer tan. Tangerine-lensed sunglasses cut down on the glare. Gwen's outfit remained basic black, but the concert T-shirt was new and bore the name of a band Sabrina had never heard of before, Great Big Sea. Despite Gwen's enthusiasm about coming along as a member of the search party, she was easily distracted.

Alberto wore a crew-neck pullover and jean shorts. His dark, curly hair gleamed in the sun. He also had a tendency to walk closer to Gwen than he did Sabrina. "That's not too far," he went on. "We can take a bus and—"

Gwen cut him off with a squeal of pure excitement. "Sabrina, look!" She pointed.

Sabrina looked, kind of irritated with Gwen for getting so easily sidetracked. She couldn't see what had excited Gwen so much because the crowd in the piazza ahead was too big. She did hear the sound of water, though.

"The Trevi!" Gwen yelped. She grabbed Sabrina's hand and yanked her across the street, narrowly avoiding the traffic.

Alberto was trapped by the changing light.

Gwen took charge, pushing and twisting her way through the thronging crowd. The sound of water grew steadily louder. Then they were at the Trevi Fountain, and Sabrina couldn't believe how beautiful it was.

The fountain featured King Neptune from Roman mythology standing on a shell chariot pulled by winged horses who in turn were led by tritons, half-men and half-fish. The fountain's waters pooled around the large rocks the statues stood on. The fountain was too incredible to be dwarfed by the faded gray hulk of the building behind it.

"Have you seen *Three Coins in the Fountain?*" Gwen asked.

Sabrina nodded, too stunned for words. Aunt Zelda had recommended the movie to her before she'd left on her trip, and the fountain scene had captured her imagination. Especially the part about the spirit in the fountain who would make sure anyone who tossed a coin in the fountain returned to Rome for another visit.

"We have to make a wish," she told the other girl. They dug in their purses and found coins. Then they stood with their backs to the fountain. Sabrina wished, then threw the coin back over her shoulder. She turned around in time to see it splash into the fountain. Hopeful, she tried the locket. It remained locked.

"Mine didn't come true either," Gwen said sympathetically.

Partially out of disappointment and partially because she wanted to get a few pictures of the fountain, Sabrina sat down on the fountain's edge. While fumbling for her camera, she peered down into the water. *Hey! That's not me!* she thought. Instead of the clothes she had on, her reflection was dressed like a Roman noblewoman.

Surprised and a little creeped out, she jumped up and almost knocked into the young man standing beside her. He'd been about to make a wish as well. Off balance, Sabrina toppled toward the pool. Before she could fall far, the young man reached out and grabbed her, then brought her to safety.

"Oops," Sabrina apologized. "Sorry."

"My fault," the young man said. He had the most beautiful eyes Sabrina had ever seen, and a cleft chin. His dark hair was cut short but a little longer in front. "I shouldn't have been standing so close to you."

His accent was American, not Italian. Sabrina glanced at him, taking in the two cameras he wore around his neck. She thought he might be eighteen or nineteen. "I'm glad you were," she said. Then she went on, flushed and wanting to clarify her words. "I mean, otherwise I would have fallen in."

He gave her a dimpled smile, still holding on to her. "I'd never have let that happen." He made sure she was standing on her own, then let her go.

Sabrina was surprised at how much she wasn't ready for that to happen. *Chemistry! You never know where you'll find it.*

"You okay now?" he asked.

Glancing back at the fountain, Sabrina saw only her normal reflection. "Yeah, just thought I saw something in the water."

Alberto came running up, looking flustered and maybe a little stressed. "Sabrina, are you all right? Is this guy bothering me?" *Keep working with those language tapes, Al,* she thought.

The young photographer stepped back, still smiling. "I think my work here is done. Enjoy your time in Rome—Sabrina."

"Come," Alberto said, "we go to the Museo Nazionale Romano."

Sabrina looked at the young photographer. "Thanks. Maybe we'll bump into each other again sometime."

"Only if I'm lucky," he told her. *"Ciao."*

Gwen approached Sabrina just as the young man started to walk away. *"Ciao,"* Sabrina called out. She was disappointed to see him go so quickly. With all the people around them, he'd disappear in a heartbeat. Then she noticed the coin he'd dropped. She knelt and picked it up. "Hey!"

The young photographer quickly turned around and smiled. "It must be my lucky day."

"You forgot to make your wish." Sabrina tossed him the coin.

He caught the coin with a flick of his hand. "What if it already came true?" he asked. He kissed the coin and tossed it into the fountain. He touched his fingers to his forehead in an abbreviated salute and walked away.

Gwen swooned. "Sabrina! He's *gorgeous.*"

"I know. Did you see him smile?"

Alberto scowled. "Too many teeth."

Sabrina led the way across the piazza, looking back for the young photographer. *The least you could have done was ask him his name,* she chided herself. *Now he's going to be a mystery man, and you've got enough mysteries.* She grew more conscious of the locket's weight at the hollow of her throat.

"Is that what you wished for?" Gwen taunted.

"No!" Sabrina answered.

"Well I did," Gwen told her. "You stole my wish. I want to talk to somebody in charge."

Sabrina smiled at her friend and asked Alberto to find the nearest bus that would take them to the museum.

The young photographer stood to one side of the Trevi Fountain and snapped pictures of Sabrina. It wasn't just that she was pretty—and she certainly was that—but there was something different about her. He had an instinct for such things. It was what his business was all about, and he was good at his business.

"Who's the girl, Paul?"

Paul turned around to find Max walking up behind him. "I don't know. Tourist."

Max looked like he'd just gotten out of bed. He wore a wrinkled shirt and wrinkled khakis, and carried a piece of pizza in one hand. He had long stringy blond hair and a goatee. He tried to eat the pizza neatly, but the cheese kept stringing out. "Cute," he said, chewing.

Paul snapped one last picture of Sabrina as she disappeared into the crowd, zooming in with his lens. "You feel like going to a museum?"

"Instead of working?" Max asked. "Sure."

"You've got cheese in your goatee," Paul said automatically. They'd been working together so long and Max had needed so much help that Paul had become accustomed to noticing things like that.

Max peered into the fountain waters, making faces as he tried to see the cheese.

Paul walked into the crowd, saying the girl's name in his mind again. *Sabrina.* He liked the sound of it. *But Sabrina what?* And since she was American from the sound of her, how long would she be in Rome?

Museums had always bored Gwen. The only ones she'd liked when her parents had taken her had been the ones with dungeons. They were in London and it had been a long time since she'd seen them, so it was possible that they wouldn't hold the same allure. She felt kind of guilty standing there beside Sabrina in the Museo Nazionale Romano's impressive statue gallery and pretending to be interested.

Sabrina consulted her guidebook.

Taking another jelly bean from the bag she carried in her purse, Gwen looked up at the statue of Bernini's *David*. This *David* had clothes on, which wasn't the case with all the *David*s she'd seen. This *David* also looked angry as he stood there poised to use his slingshot. She popped the jelly bean into her mouth and started chewing.

43

Alberto had proven quite knowledgeable about the museum, and she'd enjoyed listening to the boy talk. He'd told them the museum had once been part of the Baths of Diocletian, which had been built about A.D. 300. The museum section had also once housed a Carthusian monastery. There was more, but she'd stopped paying attention.

"It'll be a lot quicker if we split up," Sabrina was saying. "The museum brochure says they have some jewelry here that might be similar to the locket."

"Pronto," Alberto agreed, and he was gone, moving through the museum like someone who knew his way.

Gwen wasn't too keen on being left alone in the museum. She watched Alberto go, then turned her attention back to Sabrina. "Could I follow you, Sabrina? I tend to get really lost in—"

Sabrina was nowhere to be seen.

Moving around cautiously, peering between *David* and some of the nearer statues, Gwen came near to panicking. "Sabrina? Wow, that's the first time I ever got lost without even moving."

"Gwen. Up here."

Gwen followed the sound of Sabrina's voice, tracking it back to an elegant white marble statue of a woman with no arms on a pedestal.

"Smooth skin," Sabrina said, "healthy glow, but I have no arms—definite drawback." Magic sparkles surrounded her and she resumed her regular form next to Gwen. Luckily the exhibit hall was empty just then.

44

"Wicked," Gwen commented, suitably impressed.

Sabrina glanced at the other statues. "It must have been a lot warmer back then because nobody ever kept their clothes on." She moved on down the hall, flipping to a new page in the book she carried.

Gwen hung back and quickly made sure no one was coming. "I can do that." She pointed at herself and zapped, but nothing happened. She stamped her foot angrily. "Bullocks!"

"Excuse me," a gentle voice called out from behind her.

A cold, clammy feeling filled Gwen as she turned around. In the next minute, she was face-to-face with *David,* the statue, who had apparently come to life.

"Have you seen a giant around here?" *David* asked politely.

Gwen ran at once, heading for the hallway where Sabrina had gone. "Sabrina!" *Man, I've really done it now!*

Sabrina walked among the glass-counter displays of antique jewelry, looking for anything that resembled the locket or the artwork that was decorating it. She was staring so intently at the different pieces in all the collections that she didn't see the person ahead of her until she'd bumped into him.

"Oh," she said, "I'm sorry. I wasn't—" Then she recognized the young photographer from the fountain.

"Now I know your game," he said, showing her

that dimpled smile again. "You go around Rome pretending to bump into guys."

Sabrina grinned back at him, feeling warm and tingly inside. "Don't knock it. It's working."

"Just so you don't think I'm a stalker or anything, you forgot something back at the fountain."

"What?"

"To ask me my name."

A blond guy who was obviously with the young photographer leaned across the glass display case, which held a large selection of gold rings. He made a big production of rolling his eyes. "We came all the way across town for *that* line?"

The young photographer ignored him. "It's Paul."

Sabrina thought the name fit him perfectly.

Gwen ran, frantically searching for Sabrina and trying not to draw any attention. *Like that would do any good.* Everybody was going to notice the nearly naked man who looked a lot like Bernini's *David* trailing after her.

"Sabrina!" she called out, hoping desperately the other teen witch would hear her.

David reached her side and swiped her bag of jelly beans. He poured some into his hand.

"What are you doing?" Gwen demanded, getting a bad, bad feeling.

Ignoring her, *David* seated one of the jelly beans in his sling, spun it around his head a few times, and let fly. The candy ricocheted around the room, pinging off artwork.

Gwen broke into a sprint. Things were certainly

going from bad to worse. *Why can't my magic ever work right?*

Sabrina was enjoying her conversation with Paul—and even his friend Max—right up until the point that Gwen came skidding around the corner in front of her.

The girl stopped, her face flushed. "Sabrina, we've got a big prob—" When she saw that Sabrina wasn't alone she hesitated, which was a definite clue that witch business was involved and increased Sabrina's attention at once. "—*gram*. A big program ahead of us." She seized Sabrina's arm and started to drag her away.

"Gwen, wait," Sabrina protested. *I don't want to lose this guy again.* "This is Paul and Max."

Gwen halted pulling for just a moment and waved. "Cheers." Then she was pulling again. "Come on. Hurry."

Sabrina started to object, then she looked past Gwen and saw *David* loading his sling with what appeared to be a green jelly bean. She couldn't believe it. Paul and Max came up to her, about to see *David* for themselves. She turned and pointed behind the two young men. "Hey, is that the Pope?"

They turned to look, not seeing the jelly bean that bounced off the statue behind them. *David* wandered out of view, already loading the sling with another jelly bean.

"Sorry," Sabrina said as Paul and Max looked back at her with curious expressions. "My mistake. Must have been the hat." She waved. "Gotta go!"

But she wanted to wring Gwen's neck for interrupting her time with Paul.

"Wait," Paul called out. "You keep disappearing on me."

"Trust me," Sabrina called over her shoulder, "when I want to disappear, you'll know it."

"How will I find you again?"

The possibility of him looking for her brought a smile to Sabrina's lips in spite of the problems *David* could cause wandering around the museum. "Twenty-four Via Badia—"

Gwen yanked her around the corner and they ran down the corridor after *David*. The corridor was filled with marble busts of famous people out of Rome's history.

"What did you do?" Sabrina demanded.

"All I did," Gwen said, pausing, "was this." She pointed, and magic sparks shot from her forefinger.

The marble busts around them came to life immediately.

"Man," Caesar the statue whined, "I've got the worst stabbing pain in my neck."

"Quit complaining," Marc Anthony the statue ordered. "If I have to hear one more Roman-nose joke—"

Sabrina quickly zapped all the marble busts back to their inanimate states.

Gwen looked embarrassed.

Hurrying, Sabrina led the way after *David*, catching up to him around the next corner just as he was loading another jelly bean. She reached out and snatched the sling. "Give me that before you put somebody's eye out."

David didn't put up a fight, acting contrite. Sabrina guided him back to the hall he'd come from and told him to get back up onto the podium.

"Is anyone looking?" Sabrina asked.

Gwen peeked around through the statues. "All clear."

Sabrina zapped *David* back into a statue.

"Thanks," Gwen sighed.

"Come on," Sabrina said. "Let's find Alberto and get out of here." *Before anything else can go wrong,* she thought.

Paul watched Sabrina and the other girl flee from the museum hall. She was so beautiful. But what else was she? He glanced at the statue of *David*, already starting to doubt what he'd seen.

Max crossed over to the statue and rapped his knuckles against it. The hollow sounds let Paul know it was solid rock.

But it hadn't been, and that he knew for a fact. He smiled again, knowing it was going to be the biggest scoop he'd ever gotten. He loved secrets. Especially exposing them.

And he was determined to get to the bottom of Sabrina's secret. No matter what it took.

Chapter 4

Paul fit the key into his apartment door and twisted. The lock gave grudgingly, then surrendered. He pushed the door open and followed it in, still involved in the argument he'd been having with Max since they'd left the Museo Nazionale Romano. The neighbors in the apartment building hallway ignored the argument. There'd been a lot of them over the time they'd lived there.

"Max," Paul said in exasperation, "quit fighting it. We both saw the same thing. That guy was just standing there—"

"In a loincloth," Max said. "Don't forget that detail."

"—when Sabrina points at him and suddenly he's a statue. Do you have a better explanation?" Paul gazed around the studio apartment, finding it as cluttered as always. Signs of Max and his appetites were everywhere in spite of Paul's efforts to get his friend to clean up after himself. Dozens of black-and-white photographs were tacked to the walls, some of the best work Paul figured he'd ever done.

Max hesitated before answering. "No. But that doesn't mean that there isn't one."

Paul put his cameras on the small table by the window. *Why wasn't I taking pictures when Sabrina did that thing with the statue?* He still wanted to kick himself for missing the opportunity. He hadn't missed many. "The world is full of things we'll never understand, mystical occurrences, unexplained phenomena. It's called . . . magic."

"But that doesn't make her a witch."

"Then what does it make her?"

"A really good magician?"

Paul waved the comment off. "I don't care what you call her, that was one of the most incredible things I've ever seen. It really was unbelievable."

Max pushed through the pile of tabloid newspapers scattered across the table where Paul had put his cameras. "And what do we do with incredible, unbelievable stories?" He picked a camera up and headed into the makeshift darkroom they'd built at the back of the small apartment. "We sell them for a lot of money."

"What are you talking about?" Paul asked, feeling agitated that Max was taking control of the situation. Paul had always been the leader between them, choosing the stories they worked on, and the slant they'd given them. He watched as Max shut off the regular light and brought up the red one.

"This girl is the answer to our prayers." Max cracked the camera open and dug the film out, getting it ready to process. "How much do you think Simon would pay for a story about a beautiful, young, American *witch?*"

Paul thought about it seriously, because that was his job, too. Their editor Simon could be tight-fisted with money if he wanted. But for the right kind of story he paid really well. "I don't know, maybe—"

"—a hundred thousand," Simon said.

Seated across from his employer in the *Genti* magazine offices later that afternoon, Paul listened to Simon's offer. The wall behind Simon's desk was covered with the magazine's covers. Some of them Paul had shot. The magazine was the Italian equivalent of the *National Inquirer.* "Dollars," Paul pressed, "not lire."

"Dollars," Simon agreed. He was a fat man in an expensive suit. His eyes were set too closely together to make him look entirely honest about anything. But in the tabloid business, he was a king.

Paul swapped looks with Max, knowing they were mirroring each other's excitement.

Simon picked up some of the color shots of Sabrina they'd developed from the film Paul had shot at the Trevi Fountain. He smiled and shook his head. "But you honestly want me to believe that this girl is—a *witch?*"

Paul and Max nodded. It wasn't the first story Simon had doubted they could bring in, Paul knew.

"And I've got a mole on my back that looks like Elvis," Simon said.

"Fat or skinny?" Max asked with mock seriousness.

Paul ignored the exchange. Max got Simon's goat by hanging with him during the sarcastic phases their employer went through. "What if we got you some real proof? Like video, unedited. Something you could prove hadn't been altered or tampered with?"

Simon held up a hand. "Okay, for the sake of argument, you catch this girl doing some *witchcraft* and you can prove it, then you'd have a story that'd be worth a hundred grand."

Paul grinned, knowing they had Simon on the ropes. "We'd have a story worth a lot more than a hundred grand. More like two fifty."

Simon shrugged. "Maybe."

"We'll take that as a *yes*," Max said. "Two hundred and fifty thousand. It's a deal. Come on, Paul." He dropped a hand on his friend's shoulder and helped him to his feet. Then they walked out into the hallway.

Paul felt so jazzed he almost couldn't resist the impulse to run screaming through the halls. "Max, you're a genius. With that kind of money we can stop taking these cheesy celebrity photos and—"

"You think my photos are cheesy?" Max interrupted.

"Yeah."

"Good, 'cause that's the kind of look I'm going for."

Paul headed down the hallway at a faster pace, his mind liquid, running down the details they needed to make this work. "First thing we need to do is borrow a video camera."

Max put on his best serious voice, barely keeping the laugh lines from his lips. "If she turns me into a statue, you have to promise to tell my mother. She loves art."

Hilda and Zelda stood inside the screened back porch of the Spellman home and watched Harvey pushing the mower around the backyard. The summer day had turned into a furnace, blasting Westbridge.

Harvey worked the yard diligently, pushing the mower a little faster than he usually did.

"He seems a little preoccupied," Zelda said.

Hilda looked at her watch. It was half past eleven. Usually Harvey had come and gone before ten to escape the heat of the day. "He got here late."

"I know, but maybe the split shifts at the pool are wearing him out."

"And maybe it's a redhead named Tish," Hilda said. "You haven't heard from Sabrina, have you?"

"No." Zelda peered more closely through the screen. "He does seem to be in a hurry, doesn't he?"

"Yes."

"Maybe he's got the afternoon shift at the pool."

Hilda pointed up a glass of fresh-squeezed lemonade. "I think I'll go try to find out." She took the lemonade outside and waved Harvey down.

He shut the mower's engine off and trotted across the nearly mown yard to her. His gray sleeveless sweatshirt was dotted with perspiration. "Hey, Miss Spellman, I'm here."

"I see that. Although I did wonder a little when you weren't here earlier." She gave him the lemonade.

Harvey accepted the glass with a grateful nod and looked sheepish. "I got up late."

"Oh? Big night?"

A worried look flirted with his dimples, finally rounding them out. "What do you mean?"

"You had a date last night, remember?" Hilda asked. She noticed the look in his eyes. *Oh, now that's definitely guilt.* "A certain someone named Tish?"

"Right." Harvey gulped half the lemonade. "We went to a movie and got a pizza at the Slicery."

"Have a good time?"

"Yeah. It was okay." He finished the glass and handed it back. "I better finish up here. I've got a shift at the pool this afternoon."

His sudden end to the conversation caught Hilda off guard. "Okay," she said brightly. "Just knock on the door before you leave and I'll pay you."

Harvey went back to the mower and pulled on the cord to start it. He pushed a little faster, doing a good job, but quicker than normal.

Hilda retreated to the house and rejoined her sister on the porch. "You heard?"

Zelda nodded. "Doesn't look good, does it?"

"No."

"Maybe we should look into this just a little more."

"How do you plan on doing that?"

Zelda looked at her and lifted an eyebrow. "When was the last time you were sixteen?"

"Eeewww," Hilda groaned. "And hanging out at a public pool?"

"That's the price you're going to have to pay if you want to do this right."

"That'll mean leaving all the household conveniences we have now," Hilda complained. "Antonio, Andre, Tiberius. The others." With each name she grew a little more wistful.

"It won't be easy," Zelda agreed.

"Well," Hilda admitted, "I really did like the figure I had when I was sixteen. And the new bathing-suit styles the girls wear these days are so cool. Okay, I'm game if you are."

Zelda nodded.

"It'll mean shopping for new suits," Hilda pointed out, "but that's a sacrifice I'm prepared to make." She grinned.

Sabrina sat on her bed and leafed through the notebook concerning Sophia's locket. The previous day, other than the reflection bit at the Trevi Fountain, they hadn't found any new leads. She was starting to feel more hopeless.

Gwen crossed to the window and pulled open the curtains, letting the bright morning sunshine into the room. "Sabrina, remember the other day when you were worried about distractions?"

"Yeah." *And you're being one now.* But she knew

she wasn't being nice and instantly regretted the thought. She looked up at Gwen.

"Well," the other girl said, "there's one across the street right now on a motorbike."

Sabrina left the bed and crossed the room to look out the window. Paul stood on the sidewalk beside his scooter dressed in a denim shirt left open over a yellow T-shirt and denim shorts. He held a single pink carnation in a green wrap. A smile filled Sabrina's face before she knew it. "Yeah, that would definitely count as a distraction. But here's the big question."

"Do you go with him?"

"No. What do I wear?" She threw open the armoire and started pulling out clothes.

Gwen gave her a reproachful look. "And what about Sophia's locket?"

"My father's note said to follow the magic, and Paul *was* there when I saw that reflection," Sabrina said. Gwen's narrowed eyes told her she hadn't made a complete sell. "Okay, I'm rationalizing. Is it okay if you spend the morning with Alber—"

A huge grin covered Gwen's face and lit up her eyes.

"Never mind," Sabrina replied. She selected jeans and a white blouse, then held them up for Gwen's input.

Gwen shook her head. "Sabrina, it's Rome. It has to be something exciting. You know, like Audrey Hepburn in *Roman Holiday*."

Sabrina pointed up an outfit that was straight out of the movie, complete with the pixie haircut. She posed to show it off.

"Too sweet," Gwen said.

"And my neck is about eight inches too short."

"Maybe something more Italian. Sophia Loren."

Sabrina pointed herself into another outfit, dressed like an Italian peasant. She looked into the vanity's mirror. *I look more like Cinderella's fairy godmother.*

Gwen frowned her disapproval. "For some reason that works better on Sophia."

"Scullery maid or international sex symbol," Sabrina mused. "I think I better stick with vintage Sabrina." She pointed again, zapping up a red slip dress.

"Wicked!" Gwen agreed.

Sabrina zapped up her leather backpack and started for the door. "So, I'll meet you and Alberto at one o'clock at the Hall of Records."

"We'll be there."

Before Sabrina could step through the door, Salem and Stonehenge blocked her way.

"And just where do you think you're running off to?" Salem demanded.

"We don't know this boy," Stonehenge added testily, rising up on his hind legs. "Who are his parents?"

"Maybe if he bought us breakfast first," Salem suggested.

Now is not *the time for revolting pets,* Sabrina thought. *In either sense of the adjective.* She rolled her eyes at them, but gave in. Actually, it wasn't so bad thinking she was a little chaperoned in the city with Paul. Chemistry could be a dangerous thing.

Especially when everything surrounding her seemed like such a fantasy. She scooped the pets up and dropped them in her backpack. "Fine. Let's go."

She hurried down the stairs, thankfully avoiding Signora Guadagno who would have no doubt sent for Alberto at once. Outside, she slowed down and walked through the gate, watching Paul as he turned around to look at her. If only her heart would stop beating so quickly. The smile that lit his face made her melt.

"Buon giorno," he called out in Italian. "Fancy meeting you here."

"Hi," she replied. "I hope you're not blaming me for this."

"Nope. I take full responsibility for this meeting." Paul gazed around, looking behind her. "No entourage today?"

"On my own." *As long as you don't count hamsters and cats,* she added.

Paul hesitated for just an instant, then handed her the carnation. Glitter shone on the petals, and it smelled fantastic. "See," he said, "that's what happens when you only practice your opening line. I was kind of hoping you might be in need of an expert tour guide for the day."

"I have plans later. But I am in need of breakfast."

"Yes!" Salem hissed from the backpack.

Sabrina shook the bag, hoping Paul hadn't heard the cat and only thought she was settling the contents.

"Perfect," he said. "That will give me time to convince you to change your plans." He gestured at the scooter. "Hop on." He got on first.

With only a flicker of guilt as she felt Sophia's locket warm against her neck, Sabrina threw a leg over the scooter and settled behind him. She put her arms around him and was surprised at how comfortable that was too. Then he started the ignition and they were off.

Paul held Sabrina's hand as he led her down the Spanish Steps in the Piazza di Spagna to the boat-shaped fountain at the foot. They'd driven near the Trevi Fountain to get there, which brought the memory of their first meeting to his mind again. He felt guilty about why he'd really brought her here now.

"The Spanish Steps are actually misnamed," Paul told her because the silence between them coupled with the guilt was too much. He avoided the other tourists, guiding her toward the sidewalk cafe at the foot of the Steps. "They were primarily funded by the French because of the Trinità dei Monti church at the top of the hill. It's French too."

"It really beautiful," she told him.

He nodded. "There used to be a lot more people coming here." He led her around the flower-vending carts at the bottom of the Steps and instinctively kept them out of the way of photographers shooting people lining the Steps. One of those photographers, he noted, was Max—armed with the borrowed video camera. The guilt grew a little stronger, but he pushed it away. He was a professional. "But, as you can see, they've been doing some restoration work here lately."

"That's a lot of steps," Sabrina said as Paul pulled out a chair at one of the empty tables in the sidewalk cafe.

"One hundred thirty-six. But it photographs beautifully." Paul took a seat on the other side of the table. "What would you like to drink?"

"Espresso. I've heard a lot about it, but I've never tried it."

"You're sure?"

"Absolutely."

Paul gave their order to the waiter, then pulled his camera out and showed her the views possible of the Steps. The waiter returned in a few moments and put the tiny espresso cups down in front of them. "That might be kind of strong for you," Paul warned.

"That little thing?" Sabrina shook her head. "I'll be fine." Then she took a sip and nearly choked, spluttering, "—with a cup of sugar and a quart of milk!" She reached for the condiments and started adding them. "Tell me more about your job."

He shrugged. "Like I was saying, basically I spend my time taking glossy pictures of the rich and tasteless so that once in a while I can take a picture that really means something to me." *At least that wasn't just a line.* He looked around for Max but didn't see him. "I don't know if this makes any sense to you but—"

"Sure," she replied. "It's like for every twelve

insipid stories the school paper publishes about cheerleaders and their pom-poms, I get to write a column about feeding the homeless."

"Exactly. So you do understand."

Sabrina sipped her espresso and frowned again. "Can we get some more milk over here?"

Paul laughed at her good-naturedly and summoned the waiter. If he hadn't been trying to betray her and her secret, he figured he would have been in the middle of one of the best times he'd ever had.

Salem stuck his head out of the backpack, discovering they were indeed on the ground beneath the table. And they were at a sidewalk cafe. *Purrfect!* Looking around the tables, he decided the possibilities were boundless. *And that matches my appetite just fine.* He glanced back at Stonehenge. "Ready for Operation FEED ME?"

"Sure, mate," the hamster replied. "Let's shake a leg. I'm starving."

Salem locked his gaze on the huge tray of food a waiter was just placing in front of an American couple who were obviously tourists.

The man looked at the tray, then back at the waiter. "What in tarnation's this? You call this an omelet? It doesn't look anything like the ham-and-cheese I get back home."

"Norman," his wife said, "don't make a scene. When in Rome . . ." She took a Handiwipe from her large purse and cleaned her utensils, then started cutting her pasta with a knife and fork.

The waiter shook his head and walked away.

Salem didn't hesitate about making his move. He sped across the distance and began rubbing affectionately against the woman's leg.

"Oh look," the woman said. "A kitty. How cute."

"Purrr, purrr," Salem said. Then he convict-whispered to Stonehenge who'd scampered further under the table. "Hurry up. She's hairier than I am."

The hamster gathered himself and leaped for the trailing edge of the tablecloth. He sank his claws and teeth into the cloth and quickly crawled upward. "What I wouldn't give to have my upper-arm strength back."

"Don't touch it, Dolores," Norman warned, giving Salem a hard eye. "He's probably got worms or somethin'."

Salem flicked out a paw.

"Ouch!" Norman bellowed. "I think it scratched me."

Salem watched contentedly as Dolores looked up from him and saw Stonehenge standing on the side of her plate. Her eyes went wide, bulging like nuked microwave popcorn bags.

Stonehenge waved, then yelled up at her. "Hey toots, how's it goin'?"

That, Salem figured, *is going to put it right over the top.*

The scream ripped across the sidewalk cafe, grabbing the attention of everyone in the Piazza di Spagna. It also interrupted Sabrina's conversation with Paul, who, she thought, grew more fascinating by the moment. She glanced across at the table where an American man was shouting at a waiter and the woman with him was having hysterics.

"What happened?" Sabrina asked.

Paul shook his head. "I don't know. It sounds like somebody found a rat in their food."

A cold, sinking feeling twisted Sabrina's stomach as she thought of where the *rat* may have come from. She reached down for her backpack and picked it up. Empty. She glanced at Paul. "Will you excuse me?" When he nodded, she got up from the table and started trying to act nonchalant as she went in search of the cat and the hamster.

Paul sat at the table and watched Sabrina disappear into the sidewalk cafe crowd. Other patrons at other tables were joining the American couple in searching the tiled floor.

"You having a good time?" Max asked as he stepped in behind Paul.

"Yeah," Paul said, surprised that his friend would be thoughtful enough to ask such a question. "She's really great."

Max slapped Paul in the back of the head. "'She's really great' isn't going to sell a lot of papers. Now get with the program. We're trying to make a small fortune here, remember?"

Sabrina found Salem and Stonehenge in the nearby alley. Both familiars were scarfing up the omelet and pasta they'd evidently stolen from the sidewalk-cafe table. She just couldn't believe it.

Salem and Stonehenge froze when they saw her standing there.

She put every ounce of exasperated disappointment in her voice that she could manage. "This is *so* beneath you."

Chapter 5

☆

Sabrina got off Paul's scooter at the curb near the base of the Cordonata staircase that led up into the Piazza del Campidoglio. During their ride up the hills leading to the Campidoglio, Paul had given her a brief history of the place. It was supposed to be the most sacred hill of Rome, and an Etruscan temple to Jupiter once stood there. The long, sloping steps had been designed by the famous Michelangelo.

She stared up at the square at the top of the steps and at the three buildings there. One of them was the Senatorium, Rome's town council, where she hoped to find out more information about Sophia.

Gwen and Alberto waited at the bottom of the steps.

Paul looked at her from the scooter. "Can't believe I couldn't talk you into changing your plans. Guess I'm not as persuasive as I thought."

Sabrina gave him a smile, wanting him to know she'd had a great time. "I bet you'd have more luck if you tried for a couple of hours tomorrow."

"Great." He gave her that bright grin back. "I should be done with work around three. Meet me at the flower market?"

"I've noticed a lot of flower markets in Rome," Sabrina pointed out.

"It's at Campo de' Fiori."

She nodded, repeating the name so he'd know she was committing it to memory. "See you then." She waved good-bye and joined Gwen and Alberto. Walking beside Gwen, she kept waiting to hear the sound of his scooter motor revving up as he drove away.

"Oh, he's still there," Gwen said.

Unable to help it, feeling good about the moment, Sabrina started giggling, happy when Gwen joined in. Things on her vacation couldn't have been more perfect.

As long as they found some clue to Sophia's fate in the Senatorium.

Sabrina opened her notebook as they walked down one of the long corridors that filled the Senatorium. "Did you guys have a good morning?"

Alberto walked closest to her because he was busy translating the words on the various doors and wall directories. "Very good," he said. Then he lowered his voice so only Sabrina could hear him. "But I think Gwen is afraid of the scooter. She held on so tight my ribs are sore."

Sabrina glanced at Gwen, who had heard the

exchange. The other girl shrugged innocently. *No way was she afraid of the scooter,* Sabrina thought. But she understood the feeling exactly because she'd held onto Paul the same way.

They stopped in front of a door marked *Archivio.* The words were close enough that Sabrina didn't need Alberto's translation. The door was large and ornate, and the translucent glass showed just enough of the huge stacks of books and documents beyond that Sabrina couldn't help but feel immediately hopeful.

"One of the cool things about a city as old as Rome," she said cheerfully, "they have a *lot* of records." Then she turned the knob and followed the door inside.

"I'm guessing alphabetizing is a recent invention," Salem griped.

"I just said they kept records," Sabrina replied, flipping through one of the huge old census books the librarian had brought out for them after they'd explained what they needed. "I didn't say they kept good ones."

Salem and Stonehenge shared one of the census books, each familiar scanning one of the pages, then turning to the new ones. Gwen and Alberto, like Sabrina, each had their own.

Sabrina tried to find a comfortable position in the straight-backed wooden chair. The room was large and tasted musty when she breathed in, and sounds seemed to carry forever. Luckily there were few people around, and none of them nearby.

"Look, look," Gwen suddenly said excitedly,

pointing at an entry in the census book she had. "I think I found her." She peered more closely. "But I can't read any of it. It's in Italian."

"Ah," Alberto said, "allow me to be useless."

"I've been perfecting that skill for years," Salem said.

Alberto took the book and read from it easily. "Sophia di Borgheses. Single. Fifteen Via della Paglia."

Sabrina got up from her chair and looked over his shoulder. "They have her address?"

Alberto smiled. "Here's another, how you say, *cool* thing about Rome. That street is still there."

The warm flush of success flooded through Sabrina. *Could it be that easy?* No one had mentioned finding Sophia's address in the notebook she had regarding the locket. *There's only one way to find out.* She stood and closed the book with happy finality.

"Road trip," she declared.

Alberto gave a street map to Gwen and his scooter keys to Sabrina. She stepped onto the motorbike and fit them into the ignition. The little engine caught quickly and revved up, vibrating urgently. Gwen slid on behind her.

"Thanks, Alberto," Sabrina said. "Are you sure you don't mind?"

Gwen smiled up at him. "Because I could stay with you if—"

"No," Alberto interrupted. "It's okay. My ribs need a rest."

Sabrina gave her backpack to Gwen, then waved

good-bye and pulled out into the traffic along Via di Marcello. The wind whipped her hair back under the edges of her helmet. *Only three days in Rome,* she congratulated herself, *and I'm closing in on the solution to a four-hundred-year-old secret. And I met a* really *cute guy.*

Nothing could go wrong.

"There she goes," Max said, vaulting onto the back of Paul's scooter. He pointed at Sabrina and her friend Gwen as they roared past on their borrowed scooter. "Let's go."

Paul started his scooter and eased out into traffic, falling in behind the two girls.

"C'mon," Max urged. "We don't want to lose them." He tucked the video camera up under his arm.

"Relax," Paul said, but he wasn't sure if he was telling his friend or himself. He wished trying to find out Sabrina's secret didn't feel so crummy.

Sabrina discovered that Rome traffic was terrible. Even for a scooter that didn't have to wait in line quite as long as regular cars. Of course, they traded maneuverability for a certain weakness toward being totally squished.

"Go right," Gwen said.

Sabrina paused at the intersection, not sure of Gwen's directions. Having the other girl as navigator for the trip was starting to look like a colossal mistake.

* * *

Paul peered through the cars and finally spotted Sabrina and Gwen again. They'd been driving haphazardly lately and it was throwing off his own driving. He'd gotten hung up at the last stoplight.

He watched as Sabrina turned right at the next intersection, then cruised through the light himself.

"Don't lose 'em," Max ordered, banging him on the shoulder in his excitement. "Get closer."

Sabrina realized quickly that Gwen was getting mondo close to totally freaking at the navigating assignment.

"Left," Gwen said. "No, right. Left."

"Left?" Sabrina asked, feeling totally lost.

"Right."

Sabrina slid in behind a taxi and started to turn right at the next intersection.

"No," Gwen squealed. "I mean right *go* left."

Already into the turn, Sabrina made a U-turn and headed back in the other direction, taking the left.

"Trouble," Max said, pointing at Sabrina's scooter suddenly coming back at them.

Paul pulled the motorbike over and cut into a nearby alley, narrowly avoiding getting busted for following them. He glanced at Max over his shoulder, letting his friend feel the frustration he was feeling.

"Okay," Max sighed and nodded, "maybe not quite so close."

* * *

71

"Do you know where we're going?" Sabrina demanded.

Without warning, the map Gwen was referring to suddenly blew out of her hands. "Not exactly," the other girl admitted.

"Time to ask a local," Sabrina said. She pointed at the scooter, zapping it with a spell.

"Scooter of mine,
Show us the way.
Fifteen Via della Paglia,
per favore."

The scooter, animated by the spell, tooted its horn twice then sped up fast enough to almost topple Gwen from the back. Sabrina hung onto the handlebars in instinctive self-preservation.

"What's got into them?" Max demanded.

Paul shook his head, trying to keep up with the other scooter as it roared through the traffic. Sabrina was a much better driver than he'd anticipated. Every time he was certain she was about to have an accident, she made an agile turn and skidded away from injury, sometimes only by inches. People jumped out of her way and yelled angrily.

He twisted his own scooter's throttle harder and picked up the pace of the chase. He grinned in spite of himself. Catching her wasn't going to be easy.

The dead-end seemed to jump out of nowhere directly in front of Sabrina and the speeding scooter. She tried to move the handlebars but couldn't. Her spell had locked the motorbike on getting to its destination and evidently it wasn't about to stop.

"Sabrina?" Gwen called nervously.

Sabrina spoke to the scooter. "Feel free to stop."

The scooter kept on with its collision course, headed directly at the brick wall, too fast to stop.

Sabrina would have crossed her fingers, but she couldn't do that and point at the same time. Just before the scooter collided with it, the wall disappeared. The scooter roared through the alley and suddenly went airborne. They landed hard, barely staying on the motorbike. The tires squealed when they hit the street.

Then the scooter was racing through the traffic once more.

Paul turned onto what looked like an alley just in time to watch Sabrina and her friend shoot out onto the far street. He straightened his scooter and raced after her, maneuvering around the piles of trash on either side.

Then a wall suddenly formed, blocking off view of the other street.

Max yelled.

Paul braked hard, throwing the scooter into a skid because he knew that was the only way he was going to get it shut down in time. He ended up having to lay it all the way down. Luckily, he and Max broke their fall by landing on a pile of boxes filled with rotting fruit.

Forcing himself into a sitting position, Paul brushed rotted fruit from his clothing. Despite the situation, he was amused and more intrigued by the girl than ever. "She said when she wanted to disappear I'd know it. She wasn't kidding."

Max sat up, totally disgusted. "Okay, *that* we should have gotten on tape."

But Paul knew they hadn't. Max had been too busy hanging onto him during the chase through the traffic. He pointed at his friend's face. "Hey Max, you've got a little something in your goatee."

Max glared, then threw a piece of fruit at him.

Paul ducked, wondering where Sabrina had gotten off to, and what other secrets she was hiding.

The scooter raced along Via della Paglia, then swerved suddenly and came to a stop in front of an abandoned old building. The horn tooted twice and the motor shut down.

Releasing the handlebars, Sabrina read the address above the main entrance: 15 Via della Paglia. They'd arrived. New excitement thrilled through her on the heels of the realization they'd survived.

"Next time," she promised, "we're taking the scenic route." She got off the scooter and looked up at the building. The doors and windows were boarded up. Weeds grew out of the window boxes and small garden out front. The fountain at the side of the building had crumbled years ago and the water turned off. "I think this is what they called a fixer-upper." Some of the hope she'd been feeling went away. If it had been so long since anyone had been there, the trail she'd followed had to be really cold.

Gwen looked up at the building doubtfully. "We're not going in there are we?"

Before Sabrina could reply, Salem stuck his head up out of the backpack. "She's right. You can't go in there. It doesn't look safe."

"So you think someone else should go in there first and check it out?" Sabrina asked innocently.

"Exactly," the cat replied.

Sabrina smiled at him.

Salem's eyes widened, letting her know the exact instant the cat totally understood where she'd led him. "Did I forget to mention, someone who's *not* me?" he asked.

Salem was stuck. He had his head in a crack in one of the walls they'd discovered after walking around a bit. He also wasn't happy. Besides being stuck, he was also expected to break into a dark house. If he could get through.

Sabrina and Gwen were off scouting to find another way into the house if necessary. Stonehenge was behind the cat, shoving with all the muscle he had.

"You're a real bright one, aren't ya?" the hamster asked sarcastically.

"Me and my big mouth," Salem agreed. All he smelled inside the building was dust and more dust. Surprisingly, it was light enough inside to see around for humans' eyes as well as cats'.

"It's not your big mouth I'm having trouble with," Stonehenge observed. He gave a final shove, and it proved just enough to put Salem through the crack.

Salem fell only a short distance to the dust-covered floor. He looked around, wondering if anything was going to jump out of the long shadows around him. The front door was to his left. An elegant marble staircase to the right led up to the next floor. He eased toward the front door and went to work on the lock with his dewclaw, managing it with more ease than he'd expected.

Sabrina led the way into the building. Gwen crept along fearfully behind her. Staring at all the stained and faded draperies clinging to the walls and windows, Sabrina was fascinated. Sophia had *lived* here. She could feel it in her bones. The locket lay warm against her throat. She passed from the back foyer where they'd gotten in through a broken window and moved into the enormous kitchen, then into a grand dining area filled with cobwebs and empty china cabinets.

The floor creaked behind them.

"What was that?" Gwen shrilled, spinning and pointing frantically.

Sabrina glanced back behind them just in time to see Salem get drenched by Gwen's failed time-freeze spell.

"Bullocks!" Gwen cried out. "Sorry, Salem."

"You've really got to get your thermostat checked." Sabrina zapped Salem dry. "I'll have to remember that, though. He's impossible at bath time."

The cat looked at her in disdain.

Once they were through with the lower floor and had found nothing but ornate furniture draped with musty cloths, Sabrina led the way up the marble staircase. At the top, she gazed around in astonishment at the maze of doors and hallways. The house was even bigger than it looked from outside.

"What exactly are we looking for?" Gwen asked.

"I don't know," Sabrina admitted. "I just like being here. It helps me get a sense of who she was."

Gwen looked skeptical. "What she was, was a very poor housekeeper."

Sabrina chose one of the doors and pushed through. It opened onto a huge ballroom that must have been beautiful back when the house was lived in. Age-stained mirrors covered the walls, and a fireplace took up a large part of one of them. The wallpaper had long since faded and had started to peel in ceiling-to-floor-length strips.

Drawn by the elegance still obvious in the room, Sabrina walked in and spun around in front of the mirrors. She didn't even pay attention to them, looking up at the high-peaked ceiling and the webbed chandeliers.

"Sabrina!" Gwen yelped.

Sabrina stopped and looked at the mirror in front of her. The reflection she'd seen in Trevi Fountain looked back at her, herself dressed in the antique clothing. She moved closer to it, intending to brush away some of the dust and get a better look. But the image faded, replaced by Sabrina's real reflection.

"Let the magic guide you." She quoted the line her father had written, knowing that somehow that was the key to the locket. Glancing around the

room, the mantle above the fireplace caught her attention. She crossed the room and ran her fingers through the dust.

"Sabrina," Gwen asked, "what are you doing?"

Instead of answering, Sabrina pointed at the dust she'd gathered in her other hand.

"Soot and grime
dust of time
Take us back
to the scene of the crime."

Magic sparkles shot from her finger. She started to spin again, more slowly this time, and the dust scattered around the room.

Out of the cloud of dust came the sounds of a party or a ball. Music played, broken by laughter and conversation. Then shimmery, ghostly guests appeared, paying no attention to the two young witches.

"Cool," Gwen breathed quietly, all her attention on the swirl of dust.

Accomplishment thrilled through Sabrina as she watched the figures and listened to the music and conversation. Then something caught her attention on the far wall. Something that seemed so familiar. "Look!" she said, pointing.

A portrait of a woman hung on the wall, but it shimmered too brightly for any of the details to be clear.

"It's a portrait of Sophia," Sabrina said as she studied it. The answer was *so* right to her. "I know it! That's what she wanted me to see here." She crossed the room to the ghostly portrait but didn't dare reach up to touch it, afraid that it would disappear. "We have to find the real one." But she didn't know where to start looking.

"Hey, girl, you've really got it going on."

Hilda looked up at the trio of boys who'd approached her. "What?"

The lead guy was lean and muscular, and probably not over eighteen years old. His blond hair was styled in a buzzcut. He wore a blue Speedo and a black biker jacket, which was kind of out of place for the public pool where the Spellman sisters had been keeping watch over Harvey.

The two guys behind him wore mirror sunglasses and had flaming-skull tattoos.

"What?" the guy asked, looking puzzled.

Hilda shifted on her towel. At present, she was sixteen again, and the new lime green velour bikini she'd bought the day before flattered her figure in ways she'd forgotten. She'd been enjoying the attention she was getting so much that she had trouble remembering she and Zelda were there to spy on Harvey and his budding relationship with the mysterious Tish.

"What have I got going on?" Hilda asked.

The boy looked at his two friends, then back at Hilda. "You're kidding, right?"

Hilda tried to figure out if she was kidding or not. Having Sabrina in the house had kept her up on current slang to a degree. The problem was much of it was from the fifties, sixties, seventies, and eighties which she'd lived through, and the terms didn't always mean the same thing these days.

"I mean, you're no poser," the guy went on. "You got it *all* going on. You're money."

That Hilda understood perfectly. "Thank you. You've got quite a bit going on yourself."

"Way to go, Jonny," one of the two sidekicks said, punching the guy in the biker jacket in the arm.

Jonny grinned and ran his fingers through his hair. "Maybe you'd like to come outside? I got a car."

Hilda looked around the pool area. A volleyball game was in full swing at one end, and a teenage Zelda was captaining one of the teams, dressed in a Day-Glo orange halter top and a peach-colored pareo. Young mothers watched over toddlers in the kiddy pool. And the older kids took turns leaping from the diving board. A chain-link fence separated the pool from the streets fronting it on two sides.

Harvey Kinkle stood beside one of the tall lifeguard chairs, talking animatedly to Tish. The girl kept her red hair pulled up under a Westbridge Fighting Scallions baseball cap that looked suspiciously like the one Harvey sometimes wore. She also wore big-lensed sunglasses, and had a figure that would have been licensed to kill.

"That's nice," Hilda said. "I've got a car too. That's how I got here."

"No," Jonny said. "I mean *I've got a car.* Maybe you'd like to come out and see it."

"What is it?" Hilda asked.

"A chocolate brown 1977 Trans Am. Fully restored." Jonny ran a hand out before him. *"Smoooooth.* You know what I'm talking about?"

"Oh, I know what you're talking about. I've seen Trans Ams before. My favorite muscle car is a 1969 Dodge Charger. Have you seen one of those?"

Jonny blinked at her, suddenly losing the light-hearted approach he had. "I'm not just wanting to show you my car here. I thought maybe you'd like to go out to my car."

"And do what?" Hilda asked.

Jonny made an effort at thinking. "Talk, maybe."

"We're talking here."

He shook his head. "Maybe you just don't get it, babe." He reached out and took her by the hand.

"No," Hilda corrected sternly, "you don't get it. Just because I'm cute doesn't mean I'm cerebrally impaired. Telling me I've got it going on doesn't mean that you're going anywhere. And calling me a babe doesn't make me naive."

"You're blowing me off?" Jonny sounded angry. "Do you know who I am?"

Hilda lifted her eyebrows. "A guy who's gotten too big for his swimsuit from the sound of things." She pointed at him.

A ripping noise cut across the pool splashing.

"Oh man, Jonny," one of the other two said, stepping back, "you're gonna have to do something, man, or you're gonna give us moonburn."

"Yeah," the other guy said. "And it's definitely a full moon."

Jonny whipped off his biker jacket and tied it

around his waist as laughter rolled around the pool area. He stalked off with his head ducked down.

"Trouble?" Zelda asked as she spread her blanket beside Hilda and joined her on the grass.

"Teen posturing," Hilda said. "If I ever decide we need to be teenagers again, remind me why this isn't a good idea. And to think of all the pampering we've got waiting on us at home. Instead, we're up here baking in the hot sun. How'd the game go?"

"They beat us," Zelda admitted. "Finally. I have to tell you, I can't be a teen too long. There's just too much energy at this age. I feel like I'm about to drive myself crazy."

"I know what you mean."

"Anything new with Harvey?"

"Oh, he's definitely interested. But she's holding back something."

"Are you sure?"

"Oh yeah." Zelda pointed out the Westbridge police officer who walked across the pool deck area and stopped at Tish's chair. He talked to her briefly, then she got up and went with him.

Harvey looked after them, looking more than a little confused.

"I'm *real* sure," Hilda said, watching as Tish and the policeman disappeared in the main building.

Zelda grabbed her towel. "Come on. Let's see if we can find out what's going on. This could be worse than we thought."

Chapter 6

☆

☆

To offset the previous day's string of failures, Sabrina decided to go on a shopping spree the next morning. They started at Gucci because starting at the top of the line sounded like the right thing to do.

Standing in the dressing room, she reached out for another of the outfits the saleswomen had pulled off the racks for her to try on. Gwen had a rack full of clothing just outside her dressing-room door as well.

"That painting has to be in Rome somewhere," she said to Gwen. "I'm sure it's a clue to the spell. We just have to find it."

Gwen stood in her dressing room, head and shoulders visible above the curtain as she struggled to pull a top on. She yelped as she suddenly fell backward, out of sight.

"Are you all right?" Sabrina asked.

"No problem," Gwen answered jumping up. "I get dressed every day. Where are we going to look?"

"Well," Sabrina said, "we can cross Gucci off the list." She checked the halter dress's fit in the mirror and felt satisfied. "Ready? Claudia, Naomi, Cindy—" She opened the modesty panel and stepped through so Gwen could check out her clothing. "—and Sabrina."

Gwen stepped through her own panel in a mini and a see-through blouse over a cami. "And Gwen?" she asked, posing.

Sabrina tried to be honest without being brutal. It was hard. Gwen slouched and fidgeted. Not exactly *Vogue*. "I don't know if it's an accessory problem, or an attitude problem."

Gwen looked crestfallen. "It might be a skin problem. Don't they sell sweaters?"

A few minutes later, they tried on new outfits. Gwen had opted for a long skirt and a crop sweater.

"You just need a few minor alterations," Sabrina said. She pointed at Gwen's skirt and the hemline started to rise at a rate that alarmed the other girl.

"Sabrina!" she protested. The hemline stopped crawling. "You can practically see my drawers."

"Much better," Sabrina agreed.

Gwen studied her new look in the mirror. "I really don't think this is going to attract Alberto. I think it might actually frighten him."

"Gwen, clothes can't make a guy like you." Sabrina admired the strappy little sandals she had on in the mirror. "Though these shoes might. Are these cute or what?" She paused, then continued on

84

with her thought. "You have to spend time together, talk to him, find things in common. That's why Paul and I get along."

"Then why are you buying a new outfit?"

"Just in case I can't think of anything to say. You know how visual guys are."

"Check it out."

Paul sat in the center of the crowded flower market in Campo de' Fiori in the early afternoon and scanned the hundreds of people flocking to the open-air food market. Few vendors were still there. The market usually only ran Monday through Saturday, from early morning until noon. The threat of rain had postponed the usual hours; otherwise it would have been deserted.

The area was one of his favorites in the whole city. It was a place where he could watch people really be people. He spotted a little boy buying flowers from an old woman at a pushcart. Smiling, knowing the emotion was as much a part of the image as the picture, he lifted his camera from his lap and took a few shots as the boy completed his purchase.

"I don't know why you waste your film on that kind of stuff," Max said beside him.

Paul knew he was talking about the pictures he'd taken of the boy. "You wouldn't understand."

"Listen, if we really want to get some hocus-pocus on film, we're going to have to—"

"Hi."

Paul jumped, recognizing Sabrina's voice at

once, and wondered how much of the conversation she'd just heard.

Sabrina watched Paul, thinking about him as she'd seen him taking the picture of the little boy buying the flowers. He had looked so intent, so wrapped up in what he was trying to capture on film. Now he just looked startled.

"Sabrina," Paul said hurriedly. "Good, you found it." He scanned her from head to toe, taking in the watermelon-colored halter dress she'd chosen. "Nice outfit."

"Thanks."

Gwen stood nearby in her outfit, but she wasn't getting much in the way of attention from Alberto. "Yeah, conversation," the other witch said quietly to Sabrina. "That's the key."

Sabrina ignored her, talking to Paul. "You remember Gwen and Alberto."

"Sure. Hi." Paul gestured to the guy beside him. "And you remember Max, but he was just leaving."

Max didn't look too certain about that, but he nodded. "Right. *My* turn to disappear. Nice seeing you again."

Sabrina wondered about his choice of words, but blew it off when she looked into Paul's eyes. *Maybe conversation is overrated. . . .*

Seeing how Sabrina and Paul just kind of casually drifted off with each other, Gwen took Alberto's arm and pulled him to one side. She felt incredibly nervous, but she couldn't just ignore her feelings for Alberto anymore either. "Alberto, why don't we go over here and look at the fountain?"

"Go ahead," Alberto said. "I've seen it." He kept his eyes on Sabrina and Paul. When the other couple kept walking, he trailed after.

Gwen stepped between two flower stalls, feeling frustrated and daring all at the same time. *How is he going to know that he likes me if he won't spend any time with me? If I can just remember that spell—* She thought hard, and believed she had it. She leaned around the stalls and pointed at Alberto.

"Alberto who with my heart does play
Fly to my side on wings of gray
And there you'll stay
without delay."

Alberto disappeared.

Gwen felt thrilled. *The spell had worked!* She looked around, expecting to find him standing next to her. Only he wasn't. In fact, he didn't appear to be standing anywhere. "Bullocks!" she cried in frustration. "Alberto?"

She peeked around the stalls but still couldn't find him. She almost stepped on a pigeon before she knew it was there. It flew up and flapped into her face, insistent about hanging around until she shooed it away.

"Gwen, are you coming?" Sabrina called back over her shoulder. Then she frowned and looked around. "Where's Alberto?"

"Oh," Gwen answered nervously, "he had to fly off somewhere." When Sabrina gave her a questioning look, she just shrugged and looked innocent. She gave one last look around, then ran up to join Sabrina.

"Looks like you're in need of a new tour guide," Paul said. "Maybe I'll finally get my chance."

"You can fill out an application," Sabrina told him, "but I'm warning you, I check references."

Alberto didn't show up again the rest of the day. Sabrina didn't appear to notice it that much, but Gwen did. That night she lay awake in her bed while Sabrina slept. They hadn't found the portrait of Sophia either. *We must've gone to every museum in this city!* Gwen thought.

Signora Guadagno's loud banging on her son's door out in the hallway caused Gwen to start. "Alberto?" the woman called. "Alberto? Are you in there?"

Frightened, Gwen went to Sabrina's bed and shook the other girl. "Sabrina, wake up. We've got a problem." She explained it as quickly as she could, watching a look of shock replace Sabrina's sleepy look.

But Sabrina only pointed.

And a moment later, Alberto's voice sounded from his room. "What do you want, Mama? I'm sleeping."

"Sorry, Alberto," Signora Guadagno apologized, "go back to sleep. I didn't see you come in."

"Is he back?" Gwen asked hopefully.

Sabrina shook her head. "Not even."

Sabrina's head hurt. How could things get so whacked out? She'd been sent to Rome to figure out the secret of Sophia's locket, and everything seemed to be getting in her way. She pulled *The Discovery of Magic* out of her backpack. "Gwen, where did you send him?"

Gwen sat on the edge of her bed, her shoulders bowed and her hands fisting each other. "I don't know. It wasn't supposed to send him anywhere. I wanted to spend some time with him like you said."

"That isn't what I said," Sabrina replied. *No way am I going to be blamed for any of this.*

Salem and Stonehenge had managed to turn up a midnight snack and were busy snarfing over in the corner of the room. Sabrina didn't even think about asking where or how they'd gotten it.

The hamster looked up and spoke, food still in his mouth. "Five pounds says he's in Greenland. She's always sending people to Greenland."

"Can you remember the spell?" Sabrina asked hopefully.

"No."

"Try. Please. It's a really big book."

Gwen made an effort at recalling. "Okay. It had heart and gray and wings in it. I think."

Sabrina checked the index in the back of the book, then flipped to the proper page. She shoved the book at Gwen. "Is that it?"

"Yes. That's it. What does it say?"

Sabrina skimmed the spell, and it turned out every bit as bad as she thought it was going to. *Fly on wings . . . uh-oh!* "Good news, bad news. Good news, he's still in Rome. Bad news, he's a pigeon."

"What?"

Salem looked up, dropping the chicken leg he was gnawing on. "I sure hope this is chicken."

"Isn't there a reversing spell?" Gwen asked desperately.

Sabrina read on. "Good news, bad news. You have to kiss him."

Gwen's whole demeanor changed. She looked happier. "Really? I have to kiss Alberto? Well, this is turning out to be quite a smashing little spell, isn't it?"

Sabrina closed the book and put it away, giving her the bad news. "Not Alberto the boy. Alberto the pigeon." She pointed at the pigeons cooing and shuffling on the windowsill outside.

Gwen frowned. "You mean like one of those?"

Sabrina nodded.

"Figures," the other girl said unhappily. "My first kiss, and it's with a pigeon." She opened the window and picked up the nearest pigeon. They were so used to human companionship that none of them flew away. She inspected it for a moment.

Sabrina felt sorry for the girl, knowing the full ramifications of the problem hadn't hit her yet. *I am so glad this didn't happen to me.*

"On the lips?" Gwen asked.

"Do pigeons have lips?" Sabrina asked.

Gwen didn't answer, kissing the bird on the

beak. Nothing happened. And then Sabrina saw the full realization of what was going on dawn in the girl's eyes. "Do you have any idea how many pigeons there are in Rome?"

Sabrina pointed up a round tube and offered it. "Chapstick?"

Chapter 7

☆

Paul met Sabrina outside Signora Guadagno's bed-and-breakfast the next morning with another pink carnation. He asked her to let him take her to the Colosseum and she agreed after only a little hesitation. She felt guilty about not spending all of her time with the art books trying to find out more about Sophia's painting. But she just couldn't bring herself to stay away from Paul. Once she was back in Westbridge, she might never see him again.

The tour of the Colosseum was perfect. In fact, it was too perfect, because Sabrina didn't give a thought to Sophia's locket the whole time Paul showed her around. Even Gwen, who'd ridden Alberto's scooter, running around kissing pigeons when Paul wasn't looking didn't freak her out. Although Gwen's efforts at pigeon-kissing were seen by a group of Japanese tourists, who then sought out pigeons of their own to kiss.

The perfection ended when they walked back to his scooter and found one of the tires flat.

Paul frowned. "Man, we could be stuck here for hours."

Sabrina glanced at Gwen, then said, "Maybe I can help." She pointed at her backpack.

Standing behind a nearby pillar, Max took up his video camera and aimed it at Sabrina. He breathed shallowly as he brought her into focus, concentrating on the shot. *C'mon magic!*

Instead of working any magic, she pulled a cylinder of canned air from her backpack. "Here," she said.

Paul took the cylinder, looking surprised.

"Girl scout," she replied. "You should see my knots."

Max put the camera away in disgust.

Sabrina spent the afternoon at the library off Via Borgognona, digging through art books and portfolios till she thought her eyes were going to fall out. After hours of work, she and Gwen still had nothing to show for their efforts.

Outside the library where he'd trailed the two girls, Max waited, excitement rising when they appeared. He got his camera ready, hunkered down behind a line of trash cans in the alley near Valentino, a designer's shop he knew the girls couldn't resist.

There was also a big mud puddle nearby. While Sabrina and Gwen were standing there, the kid he'd paid off came roaring by on his bike, deliberately running through the mud puddle, then dashing away as quickly as possible.

Sabrina didn't look happy at all. Then she pointed at her clothes. Instantly, they were clean again.

Max almost yelled in delight. Then he realized the lens of the video camera was covered with the same mud that had slopped over the girls. He wanted to yell in frustration.

That night, Sabrina went to sleep working on magic spells from her spellbook, trying them on the locket one after the other, then marking them down in the notebook.

In the morning, Paul was there again with another carnation. This time he offered to take her to the Pantheon, the only building from ancient Rome that remained entirely intact. She didn't resist for long.

They held hands as he talked and pointed out the different attractions about the building's famous ceiling. Gwen spent her time on the steps of the Pantheon, kissing one pigeon after another that lined up at her feet.

The flowers kept coming, and so did the distractions.

And so, Gwen groused, did the pigeons.

Both girls were rapidly losing all hope.

* * *

Max watched Sabrina and Gwen wander through the Roman Forum several days later. He still hadn't gotten any video footage, and he hadn't even seen her work any more magic. He was getting really irritated because Paul had seemed to lose interest in the project. And in the money, which wasn't understandable at all.

After walking around most of the morning, Max got fed up. When Gwen disappeared and Sabrina got interested in a reflecting pool a short distance away, he seized Paul's arm and pulled him over.

"How do you say *bite* in Italian?" Max demanded.

"Morsicatura," Paul answered.

"Well," Max said, "this *morsicaturas!* We've spent over a week with her and nothing. If you ask me, I think you're enjoying yourself a little too much."

Paul didn't answer, his attention focused solely on Sabrina.

Max wanted to brain him with the video camera. The girl was a quarter-million-dollar story, and Paul acted like he didn't have a care in the world.

Sabrina sat on the edge of the reflecting pool and looked into it. Only her normal reflection peered back at her. She ran her hand through the water and broke the image up. "Where are you, Sophia?" she asked with a sigh. She looked up as Paul sat down beside her.

"Hey," he said. "You okay?"

Sabrina brushed her hair back from her face,

determined not to spoil the trip he'd planned for her. "Yeah, I'm fine."

"Liar," he accused.

After spending over a week with him, Sabrina knew she couldn't hide everything from him. "I go home in a few days and I'm afraid I'm going to let a lot of people down."

"Maybe if you weren't so secretive I could help you."

Sabrina grinned, making a joke of it so the conversation wouldn't take on serious overtones. She just wasn't ready for that. "But, if I told you, then I'd have to kill you. And that gets so messy. What am I going to do with the body?"

Paul didn't go for the light touch, and she really hadn't expected him to. He'd known she was holding back on him. "Sabrina, you can trust me."

She looked into those green eyes and made her decision. "It probably sounds silly, but I'm trying to find the portrait of the woman who owned this locket." She showed it to him.

"Do you know who painted it?"

"Roberto Raoli. All I've been able to find out is that he was a really minor Renaissance painter."

Paul shook his head. "Never heard of him."

"Nobody has," Sabrina sighed.

Paul smiled, that triumphant smile of his she'd first liked so much. "That's where you're wrong. Come on." He took her hand and helped her to her feet.

Sabrina studied the painting. It was of a bowl of fruit, and it hung on a wall in the Capitoline

Museum, which was right across the plaza from the Senatorium where she'd first found Sophia's old address.

"Fruit?" Sabrina asked.

Paul stood beside her, and Max and Gwen were there looking at the painting as well.

"The best part about working for a sleazy tabloid—they've got a really great research department," Paul said.

Gwen whispered to Sabrina through Chapstick-oiled lips. "Maybe it's Sophia's fruit."

"I can see why nobody ever heard of him," Paul said. "The perspective's all wrong and the color is—"

Max pretended to snore. "That's the sound of nobody caring," he said. "And us not getting any *tape*," he hissed at Paul. He shifted his attention to Sabrina and Gwen. "Let's go see if we can find the one you're looking for."

Sabrina nodded, still not believing how bad the painting was. There were more pictures down in the portrait room, according to the information Paul had found.

Gwen lingered behind the group, staring deep into the painting of the fruit. Perspective off or not, it made her hungry. Mouthing a spell, she reached into the picture and tried to take an apple.

Only her hand got stuck in the painting.

She yanked on her hand frantically, trying to free it. She wanted to scream, not knowing what to do.

Thankfully, Sabrina stuck her head back around

the corner in the room to see what was keeping her. Gwen pointed helplessly to her trapped arm.

Sabrina's eyes got huge, which only made Gwen feel more embarrassed.

"Hey," Paul called from the hallway outside, "aren't you guys coming?"

Sabrina glanced around the room quickly, and Gwen thought the girl was clearly going to go bonkers this time. Wickets didn't come any stickier than this. Then Sabrina pointed at her shadow on the wall. "Take a walk," she commanded.

Her shadow tossed her a quick salute, then marched off without her in the other direction.

"Sabrina?" Paul called. Then he hurried after the shadow, trying to catch up, with Max in tow. "Sabrina! Wait up."

Once they were gone, Sabrina tried pulling on Gwen's arm again. "This isn't working." She pointed at the painting, then suddenly shrunk down and appeared beside the bowl of fruit.

"Wicked," Gwen said appreciatively. "You're so good at that."

Inside the picture, Sabrina tried to pry Gwen's hand from the apple. Nothing turned loose anywhere. "I'm no better than you are," Sabrina disagreed. "I just concentrate more. Wow!"

"What's the matter?" Gwen asked, not believing that something else could be wrong.

"Look at your nails. We're getting manicures." Then she switched to the problem at hand. "Gwen, you're going to have to come in here."

"But—"

"Concentrate," Sabrina suggested.

Gwen did, trying to imagine how it must feel being inside the picture. Then all of a sudden, she *was* in the picture, standing beside Sabrina. "Hey, I did it. Now *I'm* wicked." She let go of the apple. "Ah, much better."

Before they could leave the picture, though, a tour group entered the room. "On your left are more still lifes by various artists," the guide was saying.

Gwen looked at Sabrina.

"Pose, pose!" Sabrina said hurriedly.

Gwen did, emulating what she saw Sabrina doing.

The tour guide did a double take when he looked at the picture.

Gwen knew it was because she and Sabrina both looked like game-show models displaying the fruit. *All we need is a voice-over saying, It's a brand-new car!*

"And on the right . . ." the guide went on, leading his group out of the room.

"Our winner today," Sabrina announced, "will take home two oranges, an apple, and a bunch of grapes." Then she popped out of the painting, making it look so easy.

Gwen followed her, taking only a moment longer while she turned her attention to the apple.

Glancing back at the painting, Gwen knew Sabrina noticed the big bite taken out of the apple.

"What?" Gwen asked as innocently as she could with a full mouth.

* * *

The guard in the main gallery gave Sabrina directions and she followed them down another hallway to the portrait room. After she surveyed the large room with all the portraits lined up along the walls, she took the door into a small side room.

Before she had a chance to look around much, she felt the magic drawing her on. There, at the far wall, she stopped in front of a large painting she almost felt she'd seen before.

"Sophia," she said, taking in the image.

The resemblance was uncanny, making Gwen comment on it at once. Sabrina might have been looking at her twin, only dressed in antique clothing.

Except Sophia had the saddest look on her face Sabrina had ever seen. She'd found the portrait, gotten one more step closer to the secret of the locket, but she'd unveiled one more mystery as well.

What had broken Sophia's heart?

Chapter 8

☆

☆

"Sabrina?"

Standing in front of the portrait of Sophia and still blown away by the resemblance she shared with the woman, Sabrina couldn't answer when Gwen called.

The other girl joined her in front of the picture, missing the turn into the small room at first, then coming back. "Sabrina, she looks just like you! And she's wearing the locket."

For the first time, Sabrina saw that it was true. In the portrait, Sophia *was* wearing the locket. Sabrina reached down for the locket in the hollow of her throat and tried to open it, hoping all she had to do was find the portrait. But the lock stayed closed. "Why does she look so sad?"

Gwen had no answer.

"Sabrina?" Paul called from out in the hallway. Then he joined her in the room. "There you are. I don't know who we were following for the last twenty minutes, but I ended up in the—"

Sabrina saw the surprise cover his face when he spotted the portrait.

"—basement," he finished. He slowly came over to stand by Sabrina. "Is this who you were looking for?"

Sabrina nodded, not really sure if she could find her voice.

Paul stepped forward, bending down to read the plate next to the painting. "Roberto Raoli, 1598. Subject Unknown."

That bothered Sabrina a lot. "She's not unknown anymore."

There was nothing any of them could say to that.

Sabrina stayed at Gwen's side as they wandered through the Piazza Navona after leaving the Capitoline Museum. They hadn't been able to find any more information about the painter or Sophia there. A dark depression had settled over Sabrina. Salem stuck his head out her backpack and laid his jaw along her shoulder.

"She looked so sad," Sabrina said, "she looked—"

"She looked carsick," Salem volunteered. "Believe me, I know that look. Do you have to bounce so much when you walk?"

Sabrina shook her head. The cat's sarcasm didn't even touch her. "No, she looked trapped."

One of the backpack's pockets shifted as something inside squirmed. "I know that feeling,"

Stonehenge grunted. "Can I get a little air down here?"

Sabrina freed the hamster absentmindedly.

"Maybe she just found out that Roberto betrayed her," Gwen suggested.

"But it felt like she was trying to tell me something," Sabrina said.

"She was," Salem stated. "Be careful."

"What?" Sabrina asked.

"I don't think you should have told Paul about Sophia and the locket," the cat answered.

"Why?" Sabrina asked. "Paul's a great guy. Besides it's not like he has any clue I'm a witch."

"So I guess all witches are babes," Max said. "Who knew?"

Paul and Max were following the two girls at a discreet distance that allowed them to talk among themselves.

"That portrait was a little spooky," Paul pointed out.

"Hey, do you think it's actually her and she's really like five hundred years old?"

"No!" Paul answered instantly, going with what he wanted to be the truth. But he knew he didn't *know* what was really going on. "I hope not."

"I still can't get over the likeness, Sabrina," Paul said. "It's just incredible how much she looks like you."

Now you know how I feel, Sabrina thought. The four of them sat around a table at a little cafe near the outer edge of the square. *Things are really weird here.*

A pigeon walked past Sabrina's backpack to Gwen's feet and she reached down slowly and grabbed it. She kissed the bird and waited. Unfortunately, Paul and Max both saw her.

That's a big help, Sabrina thought.

Gwen looked up at the them. "Ah, I was just—"

Sabrina spoke hurriedly. "Gwen's an ornithologist."

"A bird lover?" Paul asked.

"She's very literal," Sabrina said.

Without warning, a pigeon landed on their table and started flapping its wings. It knocked over their drinks, causing all of them to jump up.

"Alberto!" Gwen whispered excitedly. She tried to grab the bird, but it flew away, gliding into the middle of the square where a flock of pigeons pecked the ground. She went running after the pigeon, leaving Sabrina with Paul and Max.

Sabrina couldn't believe it, on the edge of totally freaking because of everything that had happened in the last hour. "Yup, a real bird lover."

"Sabrina!" Gwen yelled.

"Excuse me," Sabrina said, pointing in Gwen's direction. "Gotta go!" She hurried before they could ask any questions she couldn't answer.

Salem knew when Sabrina was gone and he didn't waste any time breaking free of the backpack on the ground. He also knew they were around food, and it had been awhile since he'd last eaten. A scuffling noise drew his attention to Gwen's purse.

Huffing and puffing with effort, Stonehenge crawled out of the purse and plopped to the ground.

The familiars swapped looks, then took off at once.

In the middle of the square, uncomfortably aware that Paul could see her, Sabrina grabbed another pigeon and held it out to Gwen. "Here. This one kinda looks like him."

Gwen brushed her hair back out of her face and shot her a look of pure reproach. "Sabrina, please, that one's eyes aren't dark enough and its beak is too short."

Sabrina totally couldn't believe it. "We've *got* to get you a boyfriend."

Alberto perched on the back of the chair Gwen had been sitting in. After spending nearly a week as a pigeon, he'd gotten to where he really enjoyed the freedom. At least this way his mother didn't have all those chores for him to do, and she wasn't trying to push him off on Sabrina.

He'd really started feeling a little closer to Gwen, but when she'd changed him into a pigeon, that had kind of been confusing. *Let her kiss a few thousand pigeons,* he thought. He could always show up whenever he wanted to.

At the moment, though, his attention was locked on the conversation Paul was having with his friend.

Paul had his camera up, taking pictures of Sabrina.

"Enough with the pictures already," Max complained. "This chick is leaving in three days and we don't have anything."

"It's a lot harder than I thought it would be," Paul replied.

"Pretending to like her, or getting her to do a little magic for the camera?"

Alberto felt himself growing increasingly angry. Sabrina was a very nice girl, not the girl he really wanted, but not someone for these two to hurt. He flapped his wings, stretching them in preparation.

"Who says I'm pretending?" Paul asked.

"Well, I hope you are," Max told him, "because she's not going to be fond of you when she finds out you were scammin' her to make a bundle."

Paul nodded. "You're probably right."

"So are we still doing this?"

"Yeah, we're still doin' it." Paul didn't sound especially happy about the prospect.

"Good, because I have got a plan that should solve—"

Unable to take any more of the planned treacheries by the two, Alberto flew into action. He flapped his wings and landed on Paul's head, digging his claws into the young man's hair.

"Hey!" Paul yelled. "Get off me!" He tried to push Alberto away, but the pigeon hung on fiercely.

Hearing Paul's yell, Sabrina looked up in time to see the pigeon sitting on his head, beating him with its flapping wings. She looked at Gwen.

"Alberto!" they said together, then ran back to the cafe.

Max rolled up his menu and swatted at the pigeon, hitting Paul instead.

"Not me, the bird!" Paul objected. "Hit the bird!"

Sabrina and Gwen got there at the same time, both reaching for the bird. Sabrina felt a few feathers graze her fingers, then Alberto leaped into the air and flew away. He'd obviously panicked, flying over the nearby rooftops and disappearing almost at once.

"There he goes," Gwen said softly.

Paul flopped back in his chair and breathed a big sigh of relief.

Sabrina looked at him, feeling sorry for him at once. His hair was in wild disarray, and there was something shiny at the top. Something—

"Hey, buddy," Max said, peering at the top of Paul's head, "you might wanna wash your hair."

Despite the fact that Alberto had attacked Paul out of what Sabrina assumed was a jealous rage, and maybe to get back for Gwen turning him into a pigeon, Sabrina almost lost it. She looked away from Paul before she cracked up and ended up locking eyes with Gwen, which was *absolutely* no help at all.

Salem and Stonehenge sat patiently back out of sight on the cafe's kitchen shelf. They'd sneaked in with the best skills both familiars had developed over years of clandestine plotting.

Salem was actually having a good time with the hamster, even if he was a surly little rodent who talked funny and craved bangers and mash. And

Stonehenge had the disgusting tendency to reject really, really good plans, not appreciating the thought that went into them at all. The cat watched as a flying disk of pizza dough flew up to their eye level, tossed by the chef.

"What makes you think I'm going' for a ride on one of those?" Stonehenge asked.

Irritated and hungry, Salem looked at the hamster and bared a fang. "Ever hear of a little thing called teeth?"

Stonehenge glared back at him, not backing down a fraction of an inch. "Ever hear of a little thing called a breath mint?"

A waiter picked up a finished pizza from the table below and walked past their position with the tray resting on his shoulder. The smell made Salem's mouth water, and he didn't think the hamster could resist. He crouched back out of sight.

Then Stonehenge ran and leaped over the edge. "Geronimo!" the little hamster yelled as he dropped.

Salem couldn't see what happened, but he heard the wet *splat!* just fine. He licked his chops in anticipation.

Stonehenge lay spread across the pizza, smelling it and knowing there was no better place to be. Then he spotted Gwen and Sabrina at their table and dug down into the sauce a little deeper, hoping the two witches didn't spot him.

With a flourish, the waiter put the pizza on a table surrounded by a large family making proper appreciative noises.

The waiter evidently figured he wasn't going to make much of a tip, because he acted disdainful about the whole delivery. "One pizza," the waiter said. "With everything."

Stonehenge lifted his head from the melted cheese and looked around at the family, who recoiled in surprise. "And he means everything," the hamster told them.

Sabrina's attention was pulled to a table nearby where a family was yelling at a waiter, who looked totally embarrassed. Mumbling apologies, the waiter hurried past Sabrina, trying his best to cover the pizza he carried. Still, Sabrina spotted a patch of familiar looking fur on the pizza. *And I do mean* familiar *looking,* she thought.

"Weird," Max commented. "I've lived in Rome for almost two years now and never seen a rat."

Sabrina glanced at Gwen, who understood immediately. They excused themselves, then followed the waiter to the nearest alley where the pizza was thrown into the trash. They got there just in time to spot Salem come out of the shadows and start scarfing pizza down while Stonehenge struggled to clean himself.

Salem broke out into song. "When the moon hits your eye, like a big pizza pie, that's *amore."*

Stonehenge joined in, singing backup with real enthusiasm. "That's *amore."*

Sabrina walked into the alley with Gwen at her heels.

Salem looked up at them for a moment, his paw

paused on its way to his mouth and holding a load of melted cheese. He cleared his throat. "Come on, everybody, you know the words," he invited shamelessly. "From the top! Oh, when the moon hits your eye—"

Sabrina tried to think of something to say, but nothing came to mind. In addition to everything else going wrong, Salem was still going to be Salem. She should have zapped him back home when she had the chance.

At least nothing was going wrong back there.

Hilda Spellman glanced at the private detective she and Zelda had hired to investigate Harvey's new girlfriend and thought everything was even more wrong than she'd thought possible. She thought that because the detective had told her, "Everything looks jake on the surface, but it's all wrong."

"What do you mean when you say it's all wrong?" Zelda asked. She sat beside Hilda in what the detective called one of his client chairs in the seedy little office in the Other Realm.

His name was Stanley Moses and they'd found him in the Magic Pages. He was short and thin and wore a faded sports jacket over a T-shirt that had seen better days. He needed a haircut. He wasn't exactly what Hilda thought of when she thought of a detective. Tom Selleck was a great looking detective.

Moses shoved a yellow file folder over to the sisters. It was very thin. "The girl's got no history."

"She's only about seventeen," Hilda said. "That's not much time to have a lot of history."

"Evidently she's got some." Moses sat on the other side of the gun-metal gray desk. The office was small and seedy looking. Clearly Moses had gone to great lengths to recreate something out of a Philip Marlowe novel. Pinups of antique cars covered the walls and lessened the impact of the mismatched paint. "I was searching her out through a Mortal database server I have. Came back nearly empty. Kids her age these days, they got a driver's license, a charge card or two, an internet account, a library card. Something, you understand. This girl don't have nothing."

Hilda flipped the file open and found a single sheet of paper inside. The color picture of Tish Nameth was even blurry. She scanned the information, finding there wasn't much more than she'd given the detective nearly a week ago.

"What about a police record?" Zelda asked.

Hilda waited. They'd never found an explanation for why Tish had been escorted from the pool by the police officer. But she'd never come back. When they'd asked Harvey how things were going with Tish, he'd been guarded, saying she'd gotten a better job somewhere else. Both sisters had agreed that Harvey was probably still seeing her. But he was looking tense himself these days.

"That's possible," Moses admitted. "I started snooping around juvie records because of what you told me. They seal those records, you know."

Hilda didn't know, but she accepted that. The

Witches Council wasn't quite so forgiving. She knew *that* from personal experience.

"I got a friend works in the division," Moses said. "Usually, I can get a sniff of what's going on, you know." He shrugged. "Got a few favors owed to me. I can at least figure out what a kid's been doing, maybe get a list of who he or she's been hanging with. But with this kid I get *nada*. They got 'em sealed up really tight." He leaned forward across the desk.

"I can stay on the job," Moses offered. "Nose around a little more. I keep pushing, something's bound to pop."

"Do that," Zelda said. "But keep a low profile. We don't want Harvey to know."

"Harvey?" Moses shook his head. "Kid's a little slow, you know, but I like him. Good kid. Usually happens to them."

"What?" Hilda asked.

"They fall for the wrong babe," Moses confided. "A girl who has a cash register where her heart ought to be, and a figure so neat it ought to belong in an accountant's ledger. Get their heart broke, maybe their head. Then they still learn slow." He shook his head. "Ask me how I know."

Hilda passed on the offer. "Stay on the job. We don't want Harvey getting his head or his heart broke."

"I'll do what I can."

The sisters paid him and walked out to the street where they'd left their car. "With this kid he gets *nada,"* Hilda repeated, but it didn't sound any better out in the open in the morning sun beaming down over Westbridge.

"We can't tell Sabrina."

"No," Hilda agreed as she got into the car. "At least she's not in any potential danger."

113

Chapter 9

☆

"Okay," Max said, "here's my plan—"

Paul watched his friend glance over his shoulder as they walked, making sure Sabrina and Gwen couldn't overhear them. Paul ran his fingers through his wet hair, his mind preoccupied with what the pigeon had done. All in all, it had been a pretty horrible experience. "Are you sure it's all gone?"

Max made a show of looking at his hair again. "I'm sure. I want you to crash your scooter into the river."

That caught Paul's attention. "What?"

"We've got to do something big," Max replied. "Trust me, she'd never let anything happen to you. One little point from her finger and you're floating and I'm capturing the whole thing for posterity."

"Forget it," Paul said. He was getting really

uncomfortable about the subject of Sabrina. He liked her a lot, and it wasn't an act. "There's no way."

"Fine, I'll do it. But then *you* have to get it on tape. And *you* have to make sure she's there to save me." Max handed the video camera over. "Six o'clock. Pont Sant'Angelo. Don't be late." He turned and waved to the girls. "Hey, I'll see you guys tomorrow. I've got to go out on assignment. *Ciao.*" He dropped onto his waiting scooter and left.

Sabrina glanced at Paul, who stood near his scooter waiting for her. Alberto's borrowed scooter leaned next to it.

Gwen turned to Sabrina as they drew even with Paul. "I should probably go too. Wash out my knickers, write some postcards—" She whispered loud enough for both of them to hear. "And let you two be alone."

"Thanks for not being too obvious," Sabrina replied.

Gwen smiled and waved good-bye to Paul, then climbed onto Alberto's scooter.

"Wait," Sabrina called, remembering the weight of the backpack across her shoulders. She slid it off and handed it over to Gwen. "No chaperones this time."

Gwen pulled it on and drove away, weaving awkwardly through the traffic.

Sabrina glanced back at Paul, who smiled broadly.

He shifted the video camera he held from hand to hand. "Looks like it's just you and me," he said.

A little while later, Sabrina finished the gelato Paul had bought for her while they strolled. He was amazed at how close he'd gotten to her over the last few days. He'd been practiced at keeping himself distant for so long, trying to figure out so many answers. *But it's like I've known her all my life.*

They'd ended up at Pont Sant'Angelo after sightseeing for a time, and he felt kind of guilty about that because he knew Max was lurking around somewhere. The bridge had been reduced to pedestrian traffic only back in the 1960s, Paul knew, and spanned the Tiber River swirling beneath them. Statues by Bernini lined the walkway.

He put the last of his cone in his mouth and chewed, realizing at once that he'd taken too big a bite.

Sabrina rescued him with a napkin, wiping his chin. She looked up at him. "So why Rome?"

"What do you mean?" he asked.

"We've got lots of cheesy tabloids back home that need photographers. Why stay here?"

He shrugged, not really wanting to get into it. "No real reason. I just like it."

"Liar," she told him.

"You always this perceptive?" Spotting two old men on the side of the bridge playing chess, he lifted his camera and snapped off a few frames. He knew she was still waiting for an answer, however, and he found he couldn't hold back any more. "I was adopted when I was about two by this great couple. But when they died a couple of years ago, I found out I'm not Irish like I always thought growing up. I'm Italian." He took a picture of two women who stood close together, laughing. "So, when I take my pictures I think maybe one of those old guys is my grandfather. Maybe that woman over there is my sister. I guess I'm just searching for a past."

"Like me with Sophia."

He thought about it about it for a moment. "Yeah, like you with Sophia."

A nearby church tower suddenly chimed six o'clock. Sabrina looked up at the tower, but Paul looked at the bank where Max was supposed to be and saw the guy standing there giving him a thumbs-up. Paul hesitated for a moment, then took out the video camera.

Max pulled his scooter back, getting ready to take a quarter-million-dollar run at the Tiber River.

"What's the matter?" Sabrina asked, looking at Paul with concern. "Are you okay?"

He glanced at Max again, almost in position now. And Sabrina would see him clearly. "Yeah, I'm fine." He reached down for her hand, making his decision on the spot. "Come on!" He led her across the bridge at a run, never looking back.

Max had to admit to himself that he was a little afraid as he twisted the scooter's throttle back and shot out into the river. But he felt certain Sabrina would save him. *Won't she?* Before he could answer himself, he splashed into the Tiber.

Then the water closed over his head and he had to start swimming. *So much for her saving me!* When he broke the surface, he glanced up at the bridge angrily. He was going to yell up to Paul, but he and Sabrina were already gone.

He floated on his back and started swimming for the bank as excited tourists rushed down to help rescue him. *Oh man, a quarter of a million dollars. Paul has really lost it.*

"Let me see," Sabrina begged.

"Patience," Paul said. He stood behind her, his fingers warm over her eyes as he kept her from seeing. "Just another couple of seconds. I want it to be perfect."

Sabrina couldn't bear the suspense. "Please?"

"Okay, ready," he took his hands away. "Open your eyes."

Sabrina did, blinking against the unaccustomed glare for a moment. Then she saw it. Sunset reached out for all of Rome ahead of her, gathering the ancient city into its gold-and-red gossamer caress and lighting the marble around them with hidden fires that were absolutely glorious.

"It's beautiful," Sabrina breathed, sorry she didn't have the words to say more. The view deserved it.

"My favorite view in the entire world," Paul told her in a low voice. "It's nice to finally be able to share it with someone."

She felt him put his arms around her and enjoyed

the strength and warmth he offered. She leaned back against his chest and put her arms over his. They finished watching the sunset together, and Sabrina didn't think anything could have been more perfect.

Except for maybe dinner that night, Sabrina amended later. She sat at a corner table of an outdoor restaurant. Violins played, their sound rolling out over the open area.

"Thanks for helping me out," she told him, "and showing me the city."

Paul smiled at her and shrugged. "I don't know. I think I've been more distracting than helpful."

She picked up her glass of mineral water and offered it to him in a toast. "Then here's to distractions."

He clinked his glass against hers. "Can you stand one more?" he asked innocently. "Distraction?"

"I think so," Sabrina replied, looking into those green eyes so bright in the moonlight. "I have a pretty high tolerance."

Slowly, Paul leaned in and kissed her. And it totally took her breath away.

Gwen stared up at the full moon hanging above the Guadagno house and wondered where Sabrina was. *Probably having the time of her life.* Reluctantly, she gazed back at the pigeons grouped on the ledge by the window box. She sighed, picked one up, and kissed it.

Nothing. That was just her luck, wasn't it?

* * *

Max stood shivering in the cold as the tow truck pulled his scooter from the Tiber River. He had a blanket draped across his shoulders but it didn't do much good.

Paul, old buddy, he thought, *we've been through a lot of things together, but a quarter-million dollars is way more than I've seen any friendship worth.*

Now it was time for some real scheming.

Complete chaos reigned in the upscale restaurant. People ran back and forth and screamed, the sounds and sights blasting through the windows in bits and pieces.

Salem watched it all in satisfied contentment from the back of the restaurant. He munched on a string of pasta, slurping it from the bowl in front of him. Without warning, he found himself muzzle-to-muzzle with Stonehenge. The hamster was slurping the same piece of pasta.

"Ahh!" Salem screamed. "Get away from me!"

"Blech!" Stonehenge spat. "Talk about cat got your tongue."

"You think I did that on purpose?"

Stonehenge glared at him. "I see how you look at me."

Salem bristled, the meal forgotten for the moment while the argument between the familiars ensued, louder even than the pandemonium going on around them.

Sabrina waved good-bye to Paul from the gate at the Guadagno house. When he was gone, she let herself into the house and went to her room. Gwen was still kissing pigeons in the window when she got there.

"Sabrina," Gwen exclaimed, getting to her feet with obvious relief, "you're back. What happened?"

Sabrina figured the other girl was more relieved about getting a break from kissing pigeons than in seeing her. Before she answered, Salem entered the room and leaped onto the bed.

"Young lady," the cat said, "do you have any idea what time it is?"

"Twelve-thirty," Sabrina answered, puzzled by the white froth showing at her pet's muzzle.

"Darn it," Salem said, "I knew my watch stopped."

"What happened to your face?"

"Toothpaste," Salem replied. "I keep brushing but I can't get the taste of hamster out of my mouth."

Before Sabrina could react to what she'd heard, Stonehenge came waddling out of the bathroom.

"I think I've still got cat hair on my tongue," the hamster complained. "Oh Bri, you're almost out of mouthwash."

"Sabrina," Gwen asked again. "What did you do?"

Sabrina put her things on the bed, wanting to keep the evening to herself. At least, for now. "You know, the usual."

"Believe me," Stonehenge put in, "she *doesn't* know. So you better fill in the blanks."

"You didn't talk about Sophia again?" Salem asked.

121

"No," Sabrina assured the cat. "But tomorrow I'm opening this locket once and for all."

"How?" Gwen asked.

Sabrina had finally figured out a solution while talking to Paul, listening to how he kept looking for his own family in the pictures he took. And it made perfect sense. She hoped, because the time she had was all but gone.

"I'm just going to ask her," she answered.

"What's wrong?" Harvey asked.

Tish glanced around nervously. "Nothing." She hesitated. "At least, I don't think it's anything."

Harvey walked beside her as they made their way to the movie theater in the downtown Westbridge mall. Long shadows filled the parking lot. He glanced around, spotting only a few teenagers who were going to the movie like they were.

"What did you think it was?" he asked.

"It's nothing, really." She looked up at him.

Harvey loved the way her eyes were, wide-set and full of fun. Except for the last week. Things had changed a lot in the last week, he had to admit. "Hey, if you're worried, we can just walk back to the car and I'll take you back home."

"Why would you do that?"

"Tish," Harvey said, "I invited you to the movie so you could have a good time. Not be worried."

"I'm not worried." She paused, gnawing at her lower lip as she glanced around again. "Okay, maybe I'm a little worried."

"About what?"

She hesitated. "I thought someone was following us."

Harvey turned and scanned the parking lot.

"Don't do that," Tish begged.

"What?"

"Look."

"If I don't look, how are we going to know if we're being followed?"

"We're probably not."

Harvey didn't think so either, but he was getting creeped out in the early evening darkness just the same. "Want to go home?"

"No. I'd rather be with you." She reached out and took his hand, using it to pull him close. "It's sweet that you'd be willing to give up our date and take me home."

"Tish," he said, looking at her, feeling the emotion well up in the back of his throat, "this last two weeks, it's been incredible. I don't want anything to ever happen to you."

She pulled him along, guiding them to the ticket window. "How incredible?"

"It's just blown my mind," Harvey admitted. "I've never felt closer to anyone faster in my life."

She smiled, looking like a pixie under her short-cropped red hair. "I'm glad. Still bother you that we don't mix with your friends as much as you'd like?"

"No." But it had at first. Harvey hadn't understood why she preferred to be alone with him. He'd thought maybe she hadn't liked crowds for awhile, but she never seemed to have any trouble with them when she was around them. "I kind of like our time together. Miss the foosball tables at the Slicery, though."

She laughed, more relaxed. "Has the time been so incredible that you forgot Sabrina?"

He paused, wondering how to answer that one. He'd told her about Sabrina back when he thought they'd only be friends, not dating, not totally crazy about each other. He decided to go with the truth. "No."

"Good," Tish said, sounding like she meant it. "You shouldn't ever forget your past, Harvey Kinkle. You'd be surprised how much of yourself you lose with it."

"I guess." He stopped by the ticket window and dug out his wallet.

"Are you at least thinking about her less?" Tish asked.

Harvey laughed. "Yeah. Until you bring her up."

Tish reached for him, grabbing the back of his head and pulling her in to him. She kissed him.

Some of the other teens Harvey knew let out catcalls and started saying, "You go, wild man!"

His face flushed and he was certain Tish knew how much she'd embarrassed him. But he didn't really mind.

"I just want to say," Salem said, "I think this is a bad, bad idea."

Sabrina ignored the cat. She stood in front of Sophia's portrait. It was still early the next morning and the Capitoline didn't have many visitors. None of them were in the small portrait room. "I don't have any other choice," she said, as much to herself as to Salem, Gwen, and Stonehenge. "I only have two days left."

"But what if you accidentally change the course of history," Gwen asked, "and you're never born?"

"Then I couldn't be here to go back in the first place so it wouldn't matter." At least that was how it was supposed to work in the *Star Trek* movies she watched with Harvey.

"Oh, right," Gwen said, her brow wrinkling.

"Don't worry," Sabrina said, "I won't interfere, I promise." She remembered Signora Guadagno's story about Sophia's betrayal. "I'll just warn Sophia about Roberto—"

"I think that falls under the category of interfering," Salem interrupted.

Sabrina let out a frustrated breath. "Okay, I'll just ask how to open the locket. Wish me luck." She pointed at the portrait, muttered a transportation spell, then ran over to it and leaped into the frame. She heard Salem's voice as she was whisked away in a kaleidoscope of colors.

"I know I'm getting blamed for this," the cat whined.

Chapter 10

Sabrina recognized the ballroom from Sophia's house as soon as she appeared in it. Only this version of it wasn't all gross with cobwebs and dust. It was beautiful. Music played and dozens of couples danced out on the floor, dressed in the rich, elaborate antique clothing Sabrina had seen in so many pictures of the time period.

It looked like the ball her magic had conjured up when they'd discovered Sophia's house, but with more clarity and color. When she looked down at herself, wondering how she was ever going to fit in, she saw that she was wearing the same outfit she'd seen herself in at the Trevi Fountain.

Cool, she decided, checking herself in one of the nearby mirrors on the wall. *Good hair century.* Then she noticed the empty space at her throat. *My locket, it's gone!*

She turned and searched the crowd out on the

dance floor. After a few minutes, she spotted Sophia, who looked positively radiant while waltzing with a dashing, incredibly handsome young man who wore a sword at his side. He swirled Sophia around with skill and grace.

The music stopped abruptly and everyone started clapping. The young man whispered something to Sophia, then left her. Sophia walked to the side of the dance floor.

Making her way through the crowd, Sabrina reached Sophia and tapped her on the shoulder. Sophia whirled, her eyes widening in surprise. Before she could say anything, Sabrina grabbed her by the shoulder and pulled her into an alcove off the main floor where they could be alone.

"Hi," the teenage witch said, "I'm Sabrina."

Sophia di Borgheses kept looking at her. "Who are you? Why do you look like me?"

"Let's just say I'm a distant relative. Like four hundred years distant."

Understanding lit Sophia's eyes. "Oh, you're a witch. How wonderful. No one has ever come to visit me from the future before."

Sabrina smiled. "They should. You guys throw great parties."

"And I know why you're here," Sophia said. "You're here because of Roberto, aren't you?"

"He's one of the reasons I came. But I promised I wouldn't say anything about the future."

"But Sabrina," Sophia begged, her eyes big, "you have to."

"I really want to."

"My family has been awful. You have to help

127

me." Sophia pointed at a sour-looking cluster of people on the other side of the room that reminded Sabrina of some of the family reunions in the Other Realm.

"What do you mean?" Sabrina asked.

"You have to tell them how happy Roberto and I are going to be in the future. Let them know it's all right for me to marry a mortal."

Sabrina let out an anxious breath. "I can't believe I'm going to say this—but, parents aren't always wrong."

Sophia drew back. "Sabrina, come on. They want me to marry Lorenzo." She pointed at a swarthy looking guy standing near her family.

Sabrina didn't like the guy's looks the minute she laid eyes on him.

"But I have to trust what my heart is telling me," Sophia went on. "You believe in trusting your heart, don't you?"

"Yeah, but—" Sabrina hesitated. "You haven't already told him you're a witch, have you?"

"Of course I have. That's what my family is so worried about. See, you can tell them that he doesn't betray me. Wait here. I'll bring them to talk to you." Sophia started to walk away, then paused. "And try some of the mutton. It's fabulous." She marched toward her family.

So much for not interfering, Sabrina thought. She leaned back against the tapestry behind her—only to discover that there was no wall behind it. She fell through to the floor of the small room beyond. The tapestry came down on top of her, swarming over her like a fabric wave.

As she tried to get up from the floor, pushing the tapestry away, she noticed Lorenzo giving another man some money. Gold flashed in the man's palm as he checked the leather bag's contents.

Then Lorenzo dashed over to her side and helped her to her feet. "Sophia," he said, "are you all right?"

Knowing that the two men didn't really know who she was, Sabrina played along. There'd been something downright sneaky about the way the two men were acting with the gold. "Yes, I am fine," she said as much like Sophia as she could. "But I must be off."

Lorenzo held the tapestry back, then he and the other man bowed deeply.

Sabrina did her best to curtsey, then exited back to the ball room. *I've got to get out of here.* She started across the room, aiming for the point where she'd jumped back in time. Then she realized she hadn't accomplished what she had come there to do. *I can't. I forgot to ask her how to open the locket.* She turned and bumped into the handsome man Sophia had been dancing with.

He captured her hand and brought it to her lips. "A pleasure. Have we met?"

"You don't think I'm Sophia?" Sabrina asked, surprised.

"No," he answered. "I've spent the last year staring into her eyes as I painted this portrait." He gestured at the wall, drawing her attention to the portrait hanging there. "You are not my Sophia. A cousin perhaps?"

Sabrina couldn't answer, knowing she'd found

Roberto Raoli. *Maybe I should turn him into a toad or something equally as icky right now. That way he won't be able to betray Sophia.* But she remembered how he'd spoken about Sophia, about looking into her eyes. Anyone talking like that, they couldn't be bad. *Could they?*

Confused, she looked up at the picture. She recognized it easily as the portrait she'd tracked down in the Capitoline Museum. Only in this one there was something different. "She's smiling."

"Of course she's smiling," Roberto agreed good-naturedly. "How else would I paint her?"

Sabrina looked around, getting her bearings. It looked right, but—"Is this the way I came in?"

Roberto glanced over Sabrina's shoulder, then started in that direction. "Excuse me for a moment." He bowed gracefully, then walked off.

Sabrina tried another curtsey, this one failing even more miserably than the first attempt. *I think I'm about to invent the handshake.* She turned and looked across the room, watching Sophia on the staircase, obviously looking for her. Not wanting to be found, Sabrina ducked into the nearest alcove. However, from there she was able to hear the argument Roberto was having with another man.

"Why are you saying this, Mercutio?" Roberto demanded. "What do you have against Sophia?"

"Nothing," the other man said. "Roberto, I'm your best friend. You have to trust me. You can't marry her."

Unable to keep from peeking, Sabrina peered around the edge of the alcove and spotted the man

Lorenzo had given the money to earlier talking to Roberto.

"Of course I'm going to marry her," Roberto replied.

"Then you're a fool," Mercutio snapped. "Things are always happening around her. Strange, unexplainable things."

"What does that matter?"

"I can't let you do this."

"How are you going to stop me?" Roberto challenged.

"I can't," Mercutio replied. "But I can't be a part of it either."

Roberto seemed taken aback, the edge lifted from his anger. "What if there was an explanation for Sophia's behavior?"

"Nothing could explain some of the things I've seen."

Man, I've been there, Sabrina thought.

"If I tell you something," Roberto offered, "you have to promise never to tell anyone."

Don't say it! Sabrina pleaded. *Please don't say it!*

"Sophia's a witch," Roberto said quietly.

You said it.

A woman's scream came from upstairs, spilling out over the ballroom and causing the guests to look around nervously. "No! Roberto!" Sophia shouted.

"Sophia?" Roberto called out. He pushed past Sabrina and ran across the room and up the stairs.

"Don't interfere," Sabrina told herself. "Don't interfere." She paused, thinking about everything that was going on around her. "Who am I kidding?" She turned and raced after Roberto, pulling herself and her gown and petticoats up the staircase as fast as she could go. She followed the painter through a set of double doors into a drawing room.

Sophia's family were already there. Sophia stood in front of them, distraught.

Lorenzo stood to one side, his arms crossed over his chest.

"Sophia!" Roberto called out, going to her.

She whirled on him, holding out her hand to make him keep his distance as she unleashed her anger through tears of hurt. "How could you? How could you betray me? I told you never to tell anyone!"

"I didn't mean to," Roberto answered. "I'm sorry. He was worried about me—Sophia?" His voice broke. "You *have* to forgive me, *mi amore.*"

"Unfortunately," Lorenzo said in a stern voice, "it's not up to her to forgive. Sophia knew the consequences of telling you her secret. Now she must pay the price for your betrayal." He turned his attention to Sophia. "As is the custom, you will be stripped of your powers and cast out."

Tears ran down Sophia's face. "No! Please . . . another chance?" She looked at her family.

They didn't give in.

"To make the same mistake again?" Lorenzo asked. "Maybe if you begged for your family's mercy, they might let you keep your powers if— you'd agree to marry me, and never see this pathetic *mortal* soul again."

Sabrina couldn't stand idly by this tableau anymore. "Excuse me." She stepped into the room, causing all of the people in the room to turn around in surprise. She took a deep breath. "I know I'm breaking all kinds of rules by interfering but—"

"Who is this?" Lorenzo demanded.

"Sabrina," Sophia pleaded, "why didn't you tell me?"

Sabrina faced the other woman, knowing the anger she was getting from her was deserved. "But Roberto didn't mean to tell. He was tricked. He really loves you. Lorenzo paid that guy Mercutio a lot of gold to get Roberto to say it."

Sophia wheeled on Lorenzo. "Is this true?"

Lorenzo looked away.

Turning her gaze on her family next, Sophia glared at them, at the way they kept from involving themselves. "You knew about this? You were going to deny me my happiness because I want to marry a mortal?"

"Trick or no trick," Lorenzo stated, "he still betrayed you. So you can either give up your powers or—"

Sophia cut him off, yanking the locket from her neck. "You'd rather I honored my magic before my heart! If my power is what you want—" She pointed a finger at the locket. Light and sprinkles swirled through the air between her and the locket. "—then my power you shall have. I will follow my heart." When all of the magic was in the locket, she closed it and threw it at Lorenzo.

The big man caught the locket and immediately tried to open it. But the lock held.

"Oh, by the way," Sophia told him bitterly, "the

locket can only be opened by someone who understands and truly believes." She reached back for Roberto's hand and started for the doorway.

Lorenzo threw up a hand, pointing the doors closed.

"Interfere a little," Sabrina said, weighing her decision for all of a second. "Interfere a lot." She pointed the doors back open. "Run!"

Sophia wasted no time at all, dragging the mortal artist with her as she sprinted from the room.

"Stop them!" Lorenzo yelled.

Two guards took off after Sophia and Roberto at once. Sabrina pointed at the nearest giant tapestry and brought it crashing down on the guards. She blew on her finger like it was a smoking gun, then took off after the young lovers.

She caught up to Sophia and Roberto in the hallway just as a small army of guards blocked the way.

"Quick," Sabrina ordered, coming up behind them and pointing to another corridor that intersected the one they were in. "Go that way. I'll stall them."

Sophia turned to her. "Sabrina, thank you. Now I know why you came back." She pulled Roberto after her, but Roberto halted for just a moment, freeing his sword and tossing it to Sabrina.

"You might need it," he said when she caught the sword.

"What for?" Running feet drew Sabrina's attention to the armed guards bearing down on her with swords naked in their fists. *Not good. Definitely not good.* She lifted the sword and zapped it with a spell. "En garde!"

Immediately, the sword went into motion, giving her the skills that she needed. She defended herself easily, blocking every sword thrust. Metal clanged and sparks shot out from the blades. With the skill her spell gave her, Sabrina started to enjoy herself.

Then the guards pressed the attack and began driving her back. "Hey, watch it!" she protested. *"You* try doing this backwards, and in heels." She pointed at herself, losing the dress and zapping up a pair of classy fencing pants. "Much better." She moved back into the offensive, breaking her opponents' attacks.

The shrill sound of battered metal filled the hallway, thundering throughout the house.

Still fighting valiantly, Sabrina saw more of the guards coming toward her. Even with the spell, she knew she wouldn't be able to hold them all off. She swung the sword faster, driving the group of guards in front of her back further.

Then she stepped into a nearby balcony hanging over the lower floor. The portrait of the smiling Sophia was her only way out, and it seemed a million miles away. Moving quickly, she flipped over the side of the banister and landed on her feet in a perfect dismount in the middle of the dance floor. *Yes! Twelve years of gymnastics finally pays off.* She pushed herself up and tried to run toward the portrait.

Before she could reach the portrait, though, more guards shoved their way through the stalled dancers. She lifted her sword and started beating them back.

Then she noticed Lorenzo standing on the balcony above. He zapped the guards' swords with his own magic, and their skill suddenly got much better.

Sword fighting, Sabrina realized, wasn't much fun anymore. One of the guards swung at her sword and knocked it from her hand. The weapon went flying. Recovering, Sabrina pointed her finger at the man.

"If she moves that finger," Lorenzo called down, "cut it off."

Sabrina froze in mid-spell, knowing the man meant it. Then she noticed the cord holding up the painting only a few feet away. She pointed and zapped the cord, causing the portrait to fall forward on her. Immediately she zapped herself back through the portrait, going back to her own time.

And not a minute too soon.

Angrily, Lorenzo came down the stairs and crossed to the portrait. He picked it up from the floor, finding at once that the girl was gone.

So were Roberto and Sophia.

In frustration, he pointed at the portrait of Sophia. Her smile instantly turned into a frown. Somehow, that felt a little better to know he'd at least taken that much.

Sabrina tumbled out of the painting back in the museum, landing awkwardly on the floor in front of Salem and Gwen. She needed a shower and a breather—in any order. But the glow of satisfaction didn't leave her. Sophia's and Roberto's love *had* been true.

Salem looked at her, cocking his head to one side. "Did you bring me anything?"

Chapter 11

☆

Sabrina resisted screaming in frustration by sheer willpower. Despite her best efforts, Sophia's locket remained closed for the next two days. Now, on her last night in Rome, she sat on her bed in the Guadagno house, prying at the lid with her fingernails. "I can't believe I stood there and watched her seal her magic in here, and I still can't open it."

"I can't believe all of Sophia's power is really locked inside." Gwen tossed a jelly bean across the room, trying to get it in Salem's open mouth.

"I can't believe you traveled four hundred years back in time and you didn't even bring me a lousy T-shirt," Salem deadpanned.

"At least," Gwen said, "you were able to help Sophia and Roberto be together."

"And work on my thigh muscles. Fencing is harder than it looks." Her legs were still sore. "Do you think your family would freak if you married a mortal?"

Gwen almost choked on a jelly bean. "They'd pass out if I ever went on a date. Though my mother has her heart set on my marrying a witch doctor. What about yours?"

"I never thought so, but Sophia's family, *my* family, was willing to lose her instead of letting her marry the man she loved." Sabrina picked up the vase of pink carnations she'd accumulated over the course of Paul's visits. "But sometimes it's so hard to date a mortal. There's this giant part of you that you can't share."

"Sharing is highly overrated," Salem observed.

There was a knock on the door and Signora Guadagno entered the room, looking at the girls. "Sorry to bother you, but have you seen my Alberto? Somebody ate the lunch I left out for him—"

Salem belched, putting a paw up too late. "Who did that?"

"—but I did not see him," the woman continued. "I have not seen him in days. Up early, in late."

Just then, a plump pigeon landed on the windowsill. Sabrina swapped looks with Gwen, then Gwen slowly crept toward the window.

"Ah," Sabrina said, "you know Alberto. He's always *flying off* somewhere. You probably just missed him."

Signora Guadagno noticed the pigeon for the first time and charged across the room at it.

"No," Gwen whispered.

But Signora Guadagno waved her arms and shooed the bird away. "Filthy pigeons. *Sparisci!*" She closed the window. "You should be careful. They are full of diseases."

"Now she tells me," Gwen said morosely.

When Paul came out of the bathroom at the apartment, Max was lying on the couch looking through the playback viewer on the video camera, trying not to feel too angry. This was the last night, the last chance they'd have for that quarter-million dollars. Paul ran a hand across his clean-shaven face.

"Going out with Sabrina?" Max asked, not bothering to act happy about the prospect.

"Yeah, it's her last night." He noticed the camera for the first time. "What are you looking at?"

"Nothin'," Max answered. "'Cause that's exactly what we've got to show for the last two weeks. You blew it, buddy."

Instead of looking like he felt guilty, Paul went through some of the pictures he'd taken of Sabrina that were spread out on the small dining table. "Not completely."

Max let some of the anger sound then, totally frustrated. "I don't get you! We've seen her make walls disappear, turn men into stone. She's not your average girl."

"I know, but not in the way you're thinking." Paul had one of the goofiest smiles on his face that Max had ever seen. "Max, I really like her. I can't stand lying to her anymore."

"It's not like she's sharing all of her little secrets with you," Max pointed out.

"It doesn't matter."

"It doesn't matter that she's a witch? What are you, nuts?"

"I feel like I can tell her anything. But I know I'm lying to her the whole time and have this giant knot in my stomach."

Max snorted. "You can have it removed with all the money we're going to make. Don't blow this, Paul."

Paul sighed. "I'm really trying not to."

But Max thought he meant it in a totally different way. He followed Paul into his bedroom.

"How does this sound?" Paul asked. "I'll be honest with her. I'll tell her everything. Maybe she won't even care."

"Right. What are you gonna say? 'Oh, by the way, my friend and I know you're a witch. Could we maybe get a couple of shots to prove it to the rest of the world? Thanks, you're the best.'"

"Let me handle this, Max." Paul went back into the bathroom and slammed the door.

"Fine," Max growled softly. "Handle it your way—and I'll handle it mine." He went back to the living room and packed the video camera. If everything worked out right, he'd be needing it tonight.

Sabrina came out of the bathroom dressed in a short black formal dress. She'd fussed over her hair for an hour and only stopped when she thought it looked perfect. "Wicked?" she asked Gwen.

"No other word for it!" Gwen agreed.

Sabrina went back into the bathroom for another look, just to be certain. "It's hot tonight. I wish there was a breeze."

"One breeze coming up," Gwen promised.

Uh-oh! A chill ran through Sabrina at once and she dived for the door to tell the other girl NO! But it was too late. A hurricane howl filled the bathroom and sent everything swirling. Including her hair. By the time the wind finished with it, her hair was standing up on end, totally windblown. "Gwen!" She walked back into the bedroom.

Gwen looked positively mortified.

"Tornado in the bathroom. At least the windblown look is in again."

"Sorry."

Sabrina pointed at herself, getting back to perfect in an eyeblink. She walked to the dresser and started to put on the locket, then hesitated, wondering if there wasn't one more spell she could try.

"Sabrina," Gwen said softly, "you tried everything."

Sabrina sighed. "I know. Sure you don't mind that I'm spending my last night here with Paul?"

A pigeon fluttered to a landing on the window sill.

"Oh no," Gwen assured her. She looked at the pigeon. "I've got a couple of hot dates of my own lined up."

Crossing over to the window, Sabrina looked down and saw Paul waiting for her on his scooter. "Gotta go."

Salem stuck his head up from Sabrina's backpack where it was still sitting on the bed. "Hey, aren't you forgetting something?" the cat demanded.

"Nope," Sabrina answered. "Can't think of anything." She waved good-bye to Gwen and started out the door.

"Good idea," Stonehenge said. "I've been stuffed in here so long my legs have seized up."

"Too bad your mouth hasn't," Salem growled. "Ouch!"

Sabrina heard the *thump* of the backpack falling off the bed.

"Ow! Get off me."

"Get your bloody paw out of my mouth."

Seated on his scooter in the dark shadows behind Paul, Max watched and waited as Sabrina came out of the house. Paul talked to her, smiling, handing her the flower he'd gotten for her.

When they pulled out, Max pulled out after them, the weight of the video camera riding across his shoulders.

Hilda was enjoying a midday snack Andre had whipped up in the Spellman kitchen when she got the call from Stanley Moses, the Other Realm detective she and Zelda had hired. He'd stayed on the case for the last week, but they still didn't know much more about Tish than when they'd started out.

"Get over to the girl's house. Looks like she flew the coop."

"Well, call the police," Hilda suggested. Her words alerted Zelda, who was reading a science manual while getting a rubdown from Antonio.

"Police?" Zelda asked.

Hilda waved her off.

"I thought about going in and taking a look," Moses admitted. "But Harvey's there, so I wanted to call you first. You don't get a call back from me in ten minutes, you might want to call the police and get them—"

"Wait," Hilda said. "Don't do anything yet." *Something's weird about this*

Hilda pushed herself up from her chair, zapping Andre's spectacular creation into nothing. "I'll be there in minutes."

"You're picking up the tab. But what do you think you can do?"

"You'd be surprised," Hilda assured him.

A little while later, Max leaned up against the side of a building where he had a good view of the outdoor nightclub Sabrina and Paul had gone to. He watched them swaying slowly to a ballad.

Love is overrated, he told himself as he watched through the viewfinder. *Give me a quarter-million dollars. That'll make me happy.*

He waited patiently. *Tonight's the night.* He could feel it in his wallet.

Gwen looked up from the game of checkers Salem and Stonehenge were playing when another pigeon landed on the sill. The bird focused on her and flapped its wings, waiting.

"Listen, buddy," she told the pigeon, "I've seen you here before. One kiss per customer."

The pigeon flapped his wings again, more insistently.

"Don't get your feathers all ruffled. Maybe it was your brother I kissed." She paused, realizing what she was saying. *Sabrina's right. I really need to get a boyfriend.*

Still, she got up and walked over to the pigeon. She kissed it, not expecting anything—and nearly freaked when Alberto suddenly crouched on the sill where the bird had been.

"Alberto!" she cried excitedly.

Alberto flailed his arms. "I'm me again!" He put his hands on his head, holding it still. "And finally I can stop bobbing my head." He looked at her, then kissed her. "Gwen, how do I thank you?"

Still feeling the kiss against her lips, Gwen said, "I think you just did."

Alberto crawled off the sill and stood on the floor, glancing around the room. "Where's Sabrina?"

Gwen felt angry. Sabrina had just ridden off with Paul, and now Alberto was asking after her. "Sabrina, Sabrina, Sabrina! I should have left you a pigeon."

Alberto faced her, his look totally serious. "She's in trouble. Paul and Max, they trying to prove that she's a witch. They want to sell the story for a lot of money."

Gwen got worried at once. "If Sabrina tells Paul she's a witch, she'll never be able to take it back. We have to warn her."

145

"Gwen, you have to get us to her."

She knew he was talking about using magic, and that scared her. *Of anyone, Alberto should know I can't be trusted where spells are concerned.* But he kept staring at her with those brown eyes, looking desperate.

"I highly recommend taking a cab," Salem spoke up.

"I can do this," Gwen said, trying to convince herself as much as anyone else. "Tracking spells. They're simple. What witch can't do a simple tracking spell?"

"Four letters," Stonehenge called out, "begins with a G."

Gwen racked her brain, dredging up the spell somehow, surprising herself. "All right. I've got it." She pointed her finger at herself and Alberto.

They disappeared with a *pop* of displaced air.

Salem looked at the place where Gwen and Alberto had been standing. He had a really bad feeling about this.

"I've still got five pounds on Greenland," Stonehenge told him.

Salem thought about Sabrina out there, alone in Rome, trusting the one person in the city who was really out to get her. It was too much. "If you want something done right," he said. Then he jumped up onto the window and leaped out of the room, depending on the special bond between witch and familiar to take him to Sabrina.

And if *that* failed, her smell.

He hoped he was in time.

Gwen looked at the frozen tundra surrounding her and Alberto. He looked terrified, and really, really cold. She knew exactly where they were, though.

Greenland.

"Bullocks!" she yelled at the howling wind.

"Is he there?" Hilda asked as she and Zelda stepped out from behind the tree they'd zapped to behind Detective Moses's vintage Volkswagen van.

"He's still inside," the detective said.

"What's going on?" Hilda asked, getting in beside the detective and picking up the pair of binoculars lying on a homemade table in the back of the van.

"I was keeping watch on the house like normal about this time of day," Moses said. "Saw Harvey come up. They've been going to the movies in the middle of the day sometimes. Figured that was what was going on here. Until I saw him turn on the light and noticed the house was empty."

Hilda ran the binoculars across the three-bedroom house.

"You're sure this is the address for Tish?" Hilda asked. "That doesn't make sense."

She and Zelda exchanged a look.

Sabrina held Paul's hand as they walked around the Trevi Fountain, which was lit up by strategically spaced floodlights. She still couldn't believe she was going to leave all of this tomorrow. It was too hard to think about, and it made her sad. She didn't want to be sad.

"It's even more beautiful at night," she told him. She glanced in the fountain and saw Sophia's reflection again.

"You want to make a wish?" Paul asked. He pulled out a handful of coins and offered one to her. He kept one for himself and tossed it into the fountain. "Sabrina, there's something I have to tell you."

Thinking about Paul and his own search for his family, Sabrina knew one way she could break her own sadness. One of them could succeed in their search. But the risk—the risk scared her to death. And, once done, there was no taking it back.

"Come on," she said, interrupting him before she could chicken out. She grabbed his hand and pulled him up onto the fountain rim next to her.

"What are you doing?" Paul asked.

"Making a wish come true," she told him. Then she pointed at the fountain and they disappeared into it in a rainbow splash of colors.

★

Chapter 12

★

On the other side of the rainbow cascade, Sabrina landed lightly on a green field overlooking a peaceful valley. Paul touched down beside her, looking totally wowed.

Sabrina smiled at him. "One wish fulfilled."

Paul looked in all directions. It was early evening instead of night now, and the sun left streaks against the western horizon. "I don't understand," he said. "Where are we? How did we get here?"

Sabrina took a deep breath, willing herself to be brave. *But if I'm wrong, oh I'm so wrong!* "Paul, I'm a witch. Fulfilling wishes is just a perk of the job."

Paul continued looking around, obviously having trouble dealing with everything he was seeing and being told.

"We're about twenty minutes west of Rome," Sabrina told him. "If you drive, that is."

He looked at her, shaking his head. "I don't know how to say this—but this isn't my wish."

"This isn't," Sabrina agreed. "But they are." She pointed down the hillside to an old farmhouse on the edge of the fields below. A large family sat at tables under leafy trees, eating a meal, talking and laughing.

Paul looked at them, suddenly understanding. "My family?"

Sabrina nodded. "I think your grandfather is the big guy at the end of the table."

Paul stared at them, captivated by the unexpected sight. "Sabrina, thank you."

"I thought you'd like it," she said. "Guys are *so* hard to shop for."

Without warning, Paul took Sabrina into his arms and kissed her. The rainbow splash pattern formed around them again, and they disappeared.

When Sabrina opened her eyes after the kiss, she found they were back at Trevi Fountain. Night hung over Rome and the fountain, surrounding them.

"That was incredible," Paul said.

"The wish or the kiss?" Sabrina asked. Now that they were back, the weight of what she'd done, of what she was still risking by him just knowing, settled over her.

"Both. Sabrina, you don't know what this means to me."

"Oh, there's one little thing," she said. "You can never tell anyone I'm a witch." She wanted to tell him why, but she couldn't. Penalty or no penalty, it all hinged on trust.

"I promise," Paul said, softly and earnestly. "I'll never tell another soul."

Max hunkered down behind one of the statues on the fountain out of sight of Sabrina and Paul. He kept the video camera going, capturing every picture—and every word.

One-quarter-million smackers, here I come!

Sabrina saw the black shadow separate from the others only an instant before it launched itself at Paul, landing on his back and nearly knocking them into the water.

"Aah!" Paul yelled. "What is it?" He swatted at the clinging shadow. "Get it off me!"

Sabrina couldn't believe it when she realized Salem was the shadow. She reached out and took him from Paul's back. "Salem, what's the matter with you?"

The cat still struggled in her arms. "Quick, turn him into a yak. Send him to the outer rings of Saturn."

Paul looked at Salem in shock. "Your cat talks?"

"That's the part that surprises you?" Sabrina asked.

A gust of wind rolled around her, then she realized Gwen and Alberto had popped in as well.

"Grazie a Dio," Alberto said in a shaking voice. "You have no idea how many places we have been."

Gwen looked at Sabrina. "Are we too late?"

"Too late for what?" Sabrina asked. "What's everyone doing here?" Then she glanced at Alberto again. "Alberto! You're not a pigeon anymore."

Salem twisted in Sabrina's arms. "Sabrina, he set you up. He's using you!"

Sabrina grew angry. "What are you talking about?"

"He and Max are writing an exposé on you and selling it," Gwen told her.

"I heard it with my own ears," Alberto added.

Gwen looked at him in perplexity. "Do pigeons have ears?"

Hurt and confused, Sabrina turned to face Paul. She could tell by the desperate look in his eyes that it was all true. But she had to ask the questions anyway. "Is that true? You were just using me? You already knew I was a witch and you didn't say anything?"

Paul tried to speak and struggled to get anything at all out. "Sabrina, I'm sorry."

Hot tears burned the back of Sabrina's eyes and tightened her throat. "I can't believe I trusted you." She pushed him away and ran.

"Sabrina, wait!" he called after her.

But she ignored him and kept running, more scared and more hurt than she'd ever been.

Paul tried to run after Sabrina, but a car cut him off before he could get across the street. He watched as she disappeared into the shadows and knew he'd never catch her. "Sabrina!"

Even the sounds of her footsteps faded.

He turned back around to face Gwen and Alberto, feeling totally helpless. "You've got to believe me. I never wanted to hurt her."

Gwen gave him an angry glare. "Sabrina might be powerless against you, but I'm not."

Paul backed away. "Hey, wait a minute. Calm down. Don't do anything you're going to regret."

"I'm *not* going to regret this," Gwen told him. She kept walking toward him. "Maybe a rabbit. No, better. How about a chicken?"

"Or a pigeon?" Alberto put in.

"How about just making me a couple inches taller?" Paul suggested.

Gwen pointed at him.

Instinctively, Paul closed his eyes.

"Oh no, Alberto," Gwen said. "I'm sorry."

Paul opened his eyes, watching as Gwen took a goat's face in her hands and kissed him. Alberto was nowhere to be seen. He looked at the goat with more interest.

"Bullocks!" Gwen complained. "Why is everything always so complicated?" She grabbed the rope around the goat's neck and led him and the familiars away, leaving Paul behind. "You can't just point and shoot. You have to get the words right, and the timing right—"

Before Paul could recover from everything that had just happened, including Alberto being changed into a goat in front of his—closed—eyes, Max appeared out of nowhere, carrying the video camera.

"That was incredible," Max said. "I got everything. In the fountain, out of the fountain, talking cat, goatboy—"

Paul walked off, feeling really disheartened. Instead of taking the hint, Max chased along after him, hopping because he was so excited.

"This was better than anything I could have hoped for," Max crowed. "We are going to be *so* rich. You can take pictures all day now."

"Shut up, Max!" Turning, Paul shoved Max into Trevi Fountain and kept walking.

Max stood up in the water, holding the camera high. "Hey, what's the matter?"

Paul wanted to tell him *everything*, except he knew Max wouldn't get it.

He wouldn't get it at all.

Chapter 13

Back in the Guadagno house, Sabrina pointed at her clothes in the armoire. They floated through the air, folded themselves, and packed themselves in her suitcase.

Salem sat on the bed watching her. "You still have your powers. That's a good sign."

"Yeah," Sabrina said glumly, "but the minute he tells anyone, they're history."

"Would this be a really bad time to tell you I told you so?"

Sabrina glanced at him. "The worst."

Gwen was about to join Sabrina in the bedroom when Alberto came out of his. He was a boy again instead of a goat, thanks to Sabrina.

"Gwen," Alberto said.

"Feeling better?" she asked, still embarrassed about the whole incident.

"I probably shouldn't have eaten those aluminum cans and that dish towel."

"I tried to stop you," she reminded, "but you were fairly pigheaded for a goat."

"Thank you for changing me back."

"Oh, I didn't really, Sabri—" *What are you doing?* she asked herself. *It's about time you took some credit for something that went right.* "You're welcome."

He handed her a mangled bunch of greens. "They used to be flowers," he explained. He shrugged. "Dessert." He looked at her, taking a deep breath. "Gwen, could you do me the favor—"

Suddenly irritated with him again, Gwen cut him off. "Could I give these to Sabrina for you?"

"No, no," he said hurriedly. "These are for you. Could you do me the favor of going out with me? When I'm a guy. Not a pigeon. Or a goat."

Gwen was shocked and happy all at the same time. "Really?"

"It means a lot to me, that you would kiss so many of my friends to find me."

Gwen blushed, remembering the lines of pigeons. "Well, you know. It was pretty good practice. I mean—thanks. Good night."

"Good night," he said.

Feeling totally elated, Gwen left him there and plunged into the room she shared with Sabrina.

"It's kinda hard to explain."

Harvey sat on the floor of what was Tish's living room. He looked up at the Spellman sisters. "I came here to say good-bye, but she was already gone. I guess that cop who showed up . . ."

"What cop?" Zelda couldn't let on that they'd been spying on him at the pool. Especially since he and Sabrina had only an "understanding" these days rather than a real relationship. It wasn't like he couldn't see other people.

"It's kinda hard to explain. See, Tish's family was in hiding. Her dad helped bust up some white-collar crime ring in the midwest. The government's relocating them to New York, but they were here until their new identities were set up. The cop was around to protect her and her family." He paused. "I know it probably sounds lame, but Tish couldn't tell me everything and then I couldn't tell you the truth. I'm not good at lying, so I tried to avoid you whenever I came over to cut the grass. I know it must've looked suspicious."

"Actually," Hilda said, "we *were* checking up on you." She explained about their concerns about Tish, and how they'd hired the private investigator. "I hope you're not upset."

"No," he said. "That's cool. It's nice you were looking out for me."

"It kind of looked like you were falling for Tish," Zelda said, sitting down next to him.

Harvey nodded, feeling the lump in his throat swell painfully again. "I guess so. Don't know how much of it was real, but I really liked her. It just happened so fast, you know. She was here, now she's gone. She wanted to tell me where she's going to be, but she couldn't."

"I'm sorry."

"Them's the breaks, kid," the detective called from the front door. "Some secrets have just gotta stay secrets. No matter how much you trust the other person."

"I know. And I wouldn't do anything that might get her hurt."

"Doesn't mean she's going away forever either," the man said.

"Yeah." He glanced at Sabrina's aunts. "Do you have Sab's phone number over in Italy? If she's not too busy, I'd really like to have someone to talk to. I have some pool money saved up to pay for the call. Of course, Dad's going to freak when he sees it."

"Sure," Hilda said. "Better than that, I've got a phone card you can use. Talk as long as you like. You never know. She might need someone to talk to right now too."

Sabrina looked up as Gwen entered the bedroom with a handful of mangled flowers. "How's Alberto?" she asked.

"I got my wish," Gwen said.

"That's great," Sabrina said, wishing she could sound more excited. She opened the window and looked out over the rooftops. The moonlight no longer seemed as magical or inviting. "But who's going to make mine come true?"

Then the phone rang and Gwen answered it. After a moment, she held the handset out. "It's for you. Some guy named Harvey?"

Sabrina ran to the phone.

* * *

After an hour and more of conversation, Sabrina cradled the phone, feeling all mixed up inside. Harvey having a summer romance kind of got to her, and then having to be sympathetic when it didn't work out was confusing at the same time.

But she couldn't begrudge him. She'd been enjoying herself as well. And Paul had been so dreamy till he'd turned out to be such a—a disappointment, was the kindest thing she could think of.

It was strange how secrets had blown everything for them, including Sophia and Roberto. That had been fixed, though, by Sabrina's trip to the past. Although the locket remained sealed. And Tish, or whatever her real name was, had trusted Harvey with so much, especially her feelings from the sound of things. At least, as much as she could.

Harvey had summed it up best when he'd said, "I guess there's gotta be some secrets between everybody, Sab. At different times. Sometimes you've got to be tough enough not to tell somebody you love, and sometimes you have to be brave enough to tell somebody something that could hurt you when not telling it is going to affect things between you just as badly. There's no rule for when you use which tactic, or for who you're going to trust. You have to trust the love, without knowing how everything's going to shake out."

But Harvey trusted her enough to tell her how he felt. She'd told him about Paul. Part of it anyway. She didn't mention the part about telling Paul she was a witch.

She felt better when she got off the phone, but it still took her a long time to get to sleep.

Sabrina pulled back the drapes the next morning just as the sun started to creep over the rooftops. She hadn't slept well and still felt bad. At least her magic still seemed to be intact.

Looking down, she spotted a guy standing by the street with a bouquet of flowers. For a minute she thought it was Paul. Then a girl came out of another house and ran over to him, taking him into her arms and kissing him.

Sabrina felt her wounded heart turn into a cold, hard knot as it dwindled in on itself.

Later, in the courtyard, Sabrina hugged Alberto good-bye. Gwen stood by the small fountain.

Sabrina took a final look around, not sure if she wanted to remember everything yet or not.

"Sabrina," Gwen said, "I'm going to miss you so much. I wish there was something I could do."

"Don't forget to use that memory-loss spell I showed you before it's too late," Sabrina reminded. "The world doesn't need to know you're a witch too."

Gwen nodded.

"And remember, no matter what happens, you're wicked," Sabrina told her.

"I will. Thank you, Sabrina."

Stonehenge popped his head out of Gwen's pocket. "It was a pleasure, love. Take care of yourself."

Sabrina petted him.

"Ah, Sabrina mia!" Signora Guadagno yelled from the porch. Then she raced over to them. Just as she was about to seize Sabrina in a huge bear hug, she froze.

Sabrina blinked her eyes all the way open and glanced at the frozen woman. She looked at Gwen.

"I finally got the setting right," Gwen said.

Sabrina hugged Gwen and the frozen Signora good-bye, then walked out the gate to the waiting taxi. She took one last look down the street. Her heart almost stopped when she saw a guy on a scooter riding toward her.

It wasn't Paul, though, and he didn't stop either. She had to dodge up on the curb to avoid getting hit.

Sabrina sat quietly in the back seat as they drove by the Colosseum. Even Salem was subdued. The next light stopped them near the Trevi Fountain. She looked out across the waters and statues, and all the tourists gathered around, happily throwing coins.

"Wait!" Sabrina said as the taxi started to move again. "Pull over."

"But your plane," the driver protested.

"There's one more person I have to say good-bye to," she said, then gave directions.

Sabrina stood in front of Sophia's frowning portrait in the Capitoline Museum. Her heart felt heavy and awkward.

"I'm sorry I couldn't open the locket," she told

the portrait. "I thought maybe by following my heart like you did, that would be the answer. But I was wrong."

The silence stretched out, making her failure seem even worse.

"No you weren't, Sabrina," a familiar voice said softly from behind her.

Sabrina turned slowly and uncertainly to face Paul. She hadn't even thought about him showing up there. He looked tired.

"Your heart didn't lie to you," he said. "I did."

"What are you doing here?" she asked.

He dumped a mangled mess of video tape on the bench in front of her. "One wish," he said, "fulfilled."

Understanding what he'd done, Sabrina stepped forward and hugged him. "I was right."

He hugged her back, then stepped away. "Sabrina, your locket."

She pulled it off her neck and laid it in her palm, watching as it started to glow and slowly opened.

The glittering spill of the magic trapped inside the locket swirled in the air and shot off into the painting. Sophia's frown turned into a smile before their eyes.

Holding the locket up, Sabrina turned it so Paul could see inside as well. A small picture of Sophia and Roberto were on one side. An inscription was on the other side.

"Avete confidenza nel vostro cuore." He looked at Sabrina. "Trust your heart."

She smiled at him. "I always do." She gazed at

the portrait of the smiling Sophia, feeling totally at ease again.

Sabrina held Paul's hand as they walked out of the museum toward the waiting taxi.

"Sabrina, wait," Paul said. "I almost forgot. What about Max? I'll never tell anyone, and I destroyed the tape, but—"

"You won't have to worry about Max," she said. After all, she hadn't willingly told Max she was a witch, so he was still within her powers. "Gwen isn't the greatest witch, but she taught me a spell or two. Now if I could just remember—" She took a compact from her purse and flipped it open. A simple spell opened a viewing surface in the mirror that showed Max in the apartment he shared with Paul. She pointed.

Max turned into a cow.

"No, that's not it," Sabrina said, pointing again.

Max turned into a llama.

"Nope," Sabrina said, "wrong again." She looked up at Paul. "I hope Max is enjoying this as much as I am." She pointed again.

Max turned into a warthog.

"Wait a minute," Sabrina said. "No. That's not it either." She pointed again, and again, and again.

About the Author

Mel Odom lives in Moore, Oklahoma, with his wife and five kids, where he works constant magic involving calendars, deadlines, game schedules, practices, and works on getting his Instant Replay spell down for umpires who refuse to admit when they're wrong.

Sabrina Goes to Rome is actually his third Sabrina book but is being published first (he didn't quite have that scheduling spell down pat), so be sure and look for *Harvest Moon* and *I'll Zap Manhattan*, both coming at you real soon. In addition to his work on Sabrina, he's also written an Alex Mack book, *In Hot Pursuit!*

Mel can be reached on the internet at denimbyte-@aol.com, and loves to swap letters now that he doesn't have to lick all those stamps.